ORCH

STEFAN GRABIŃSKI was b...
(now Kamianka-Buzka, Ukraine). Grabiński's childhood was a sickly
one, with much time spent in bed reading, a habit that helped foster a
slightly reclusive nature and fed his interest in stories of dark fantasy and
mysticism. After the death of his father, a judge, the family moved to
Lviv, where Grabiński graduated from Jan Kazimierz University, studying classical philology and Polish literature. Upon graduating in 1911, he
worked as a teacher in Lviv and Przemyśl and also traveled extensively,
including in Austria, Italy, and Romania.

He began writing short fiction in 1906, and in 1909 he pseudony-
mously self-published his debut collection; however, the volume did not
meet with critical or popular success. It would take nine years before his
next collection, *On the Hill of Roses* (1918) appeared; this marked the start
of an extraordinarily fertile period for the author, who published four
more collections over the next four years, including perhaps his most
famous, *The Motion Demon* (1919). In the latter part of his career, Grabiński
focused on longer fiction, publishing four novels between 1924 and 1936.

In the 1920s, Grabiński's tuberculosis, first diagnosed when he was at
university, became worse and he was forced to retire from teaching and
spend more time seeking treatment. In 1931 he settled in the resort and spa
town of Brzuchowice, where he increasingly fell into obscurity. In 1936
he died in extreme poverty in Lviv and was buried there. With his death,
his works were quickly forgotten and were not rediscovered by Polish
critics until long after, a process that began with literary historian Artur
Hutnikiewicz's monograph on the author in 1959. His work remained
largely unknown in English until Dedalus Classics published the slim
volume *The Dark Domain* in 1993; though a handful of other English pub-
lications have appeared since, a significant portion of his output remains
unavailable in translation.

BRIAN EVENSON is the author of a dozen books of fiction, most recently
the collection *The Glassy Burning Floor of Hell* (2021). His previous book,
Song for the Unraveling of the World (2019), won the Shirley Jackson Award
and the World Fantasy Award and was a finalist for the *Los Angeles Times*'
Ray Bradbury Prize. He is the recipient of three O. Henry Prizes, an
NEA fellowship, and a Guggenheim Award. His work has been translated
into more than a dozen languages. He lives in Los Angeles and teaches in
the Critical Studies Program at CalArts.

ORCHARD OF THE DEAD

and other macabre tales

by
STEFAN GRABINSKI

Selected and translated from the Polish by
ANTHONY SCISCIONE

Introduction by BRIAN EVENSON

VALANCOURT BOOKS

Orchard of the Dead and Other Macabre Tales by Stefan Grabinski
First edition 2023

The texts translated in this edition are taken from the Polish edition
entitled *Opowieści niesamowite*, published in 2013 by Armoryka

Published by Valancourt Books, Richmond, Virginia
http://www.valancourtbooks.com

ISBN 978-1-960241-04-7 (hardcover)
ISBN 978-1-960241-05-4 (trade paperback)
Also available as an electronic book.

Cover by Vince Haig
Set in Dante MT

This publication has been supported by the ©POLAND Translation Program

BOOK INSTITUTE

©POLAND

Contents

Introduction by Brian Evenson   7

A Night's Lodging   11
At Sarah's House   23
Burning Ground   45
Parable of the Tunnel Mole   63
Before a Long Journey   77
Blind Man's Buff   88
Orchard of the Dead   96
Ksenia   109
On the Trail   116
Mud Hut in a Clear Field   132
Red Magda   140
The Loft   153
Countess Maspera's Secret   162
Szatera's Engrams   172

Introduction

S tefan Grabiński (1887-1934) was an accomplished writer of fantastical fiction. Though he is sometimes seen as the Polish answer to Poe or even as the Polish Lovecraft, a better point of comparison strikes me as French Decadent writers such as Charles Baudelaire or J.-K. Huysmans. Or, better yet, as what might have happened if Kafka's 'A Country Doctor' and Villiers de l'Isle-Adam's *Cruel Stories* had had a baby and Félicien Rops served as midwife. Grabiński is at once committedly perverse and intriguingly Weird in a highly original and personal way.

What's so interesting to me about Grabiński is how startling his stories can still seem today. My first introduction to his work came when I read 'The White Wyrax' in Ann and Jeff VanderMeer's anthology *The Weird*. That story, about a strange creature that is 'part monkey, and part large frog' which has come into existence in a chimney and which kills several people, reads like a folk tale gone wrong. It was not quite like anything I'd read before. Eager for more, I discovered *The Motion Demon*, a book of Weird tales about trains, and then the stories gathered in *The Dark Domain*, which introduced me to 'Fumes', an unsettling story that revolves around eroticism and gender confusion/transformation. These stories, and indeed all the stories of Grabiński that I've read to date, in certain ways seem almost contemporary and in others seem very much of their time. Indeed, reading Grabiński can feel almost like reading someone from an alternate dimension: as if one is getting a glimpse of a direction fantastical fiction could have, and maybe should have, taken.

The volume you hold in your hands collects a number of Grabiński stories, most of which are either previously unpublished or have been published only in expensive or out-of-print limited editions. Readily on display is Grabiński's commitment to the perverse, a certain obsessiveness that surfaces again and again among his characters, sometimes tumbling into lust. Here you will find several stories of fire morphing into desire and obsession, as well as stories exploring mental disorientation and decay. In a few others trains appear, though not as frequently as in *The Motion Demon*, and more often as a backdrop than a focus.

At play in most of these stories is Grabiński's fascination with the erotic. 'At Sarah's House', for instance, is a tale of sexual vampirism in which one must choose either to resist desire or be consumed and destroyed by it. The narrator has to decide whether to consummate his lust and become something less than human or resist and survive. Somehow Grabiński manages to pull this off without it feeling moralizing: it's not a story about chastity – sex is fair game: you just can't sleep with a vampire.

But the most interesting thing about this story is the way the vampiric character, unable to sustain itself, becomes desperately afraid. Says one of the characters in 'Before a Long Journey': 'You give off the impression of a shadow desperate to become a solid object.' That desperation haunts many of Grabiński's characters, who find themselves unable to materialize quite fully, who are haunted by their nightmares or who have a sense of not being entirely realized – who confuse dream with reality and reality with dream.

One my favorite stories in this collection, 'Blind Man's Buff', has a very simple premise: Grześ is 'passionately fond of Blind Man's Buff', but the reason he likes it is that there is 'something mysterious about the game, something that eluded the controlling grasp of definitions – unusual, peculiar, enigmatic …' That for me touches on something at the heart of Grabiński's work: a thoroughgoing attempt to embrace that which remains unembraceable, always just outside of one's grasp.

That's one thing that gives his work such dynamism, another being the unusual settings and premises of much of his horror. In the words of China Miéville, rather than writing horror beholden to the past and its tropes (haunted houses, ghosts, etc.), Grabiński is 'a writer for whom supernatural horror is manifest precisely in modernity ... the uncanny as the bad conscience of today.' Like Fritz Leiber in 'Smoke Ghost', Grabiński finds horror under stones that most writers of his time left unturned. To what extent, Grześ asks himself in 'Blind Man's Buff', can a game become more than a game? If one follows its rules carefully, precisely, can something else begin to happen, can some other, hidden world begin to unfurl? Or rather, he doesn't ask himself this *per se*, doesn't reason it out: he just pursues his intuition as he plays blind man's buff in a way that begins more and more to allow him to touch 'some unknown thing ... some strange, peculiar or unusual object' that, when he whips his blindfold off, simply isn't there. At first this delights him, but as time goes on, it will prove to be anything but a source for delight.

Curiously enough, Grześ reappears in a story toward the end of the volume, 'The Loft' – or someone of that same name does anyway. Perhaps Grześ is as common a name in Poland as John is in the United States, but I'd like to think that this is the same hapless Grześ who, giving up his games for something fleshier, ends up in an even more hapless dilemma. Or at very least that it's an alternate Grześ, a Grześ from another timeline who never discovered the joys and terrors of blind man's buff.

A story like 'Burning Ground' offers a simple proposition: someone who doesn't believe in superstition decides to build on a plot of land where every house ever built has caught fire. He's careful, he takes precautions, but as time goes on he begins to become more and more infected by the spirit of the place and by an obsession with fire itself. Lust and fire often function in the same way for Grabiński, and his fascination with each is equally perverse and intertwined. From early on in the story you can guess where it will end up, but the agony and care with which Grabiński gets there is exquisite.

In another fire story, 'Red Magda', fires constantly seem to be breaking out around the mysterious daughter of a fireman. Supernatural elements aside, much of the satisfaction of the story lies in Grabiński's depictions of the details of firefighting, which are as compelling as those found in William Sansom's 'Fireman Flower' or Henry Green's *Caught*.

'Orchard of the Dead' concerns a cemetery transformed into an orchard, the fruit left to rot since it belongs to the dead, a decision that begins to be questioned. What's surprising about this story next to the others is its gentleness – and that despite that gentleness it's difficult to forget these trees are nourishing themselves on the bodies of the dead.

'Parable of the Tunnel Mole' is one of the railway stories in this collection, though it is more a story of darkness and what its main character finds underneath the ground, and how he finally severs connection with the world above. 'Szatera's Engrams', however, takes place squarely in the railway station, with Szatera beginning to notice transient 'traces of facts and occurrences in the past', particularly of tragic occurrences, that return to our world as echoes, appearing as figures in the sand on the tracks or as strange shadows. Once he begins to notice them, he increasingly wants to 'have the past alive before his eyes, still pulsing with the blood of the here-and-now, eternally present …' Deftly muddling the boundary between the supernatural and the psychological, this is a careful and merciless study of the mental undoing of a character.

Throughout these stories and the other stories gathered here, Grabiński forges his own path, weaving between the psychological and the supernatural in a way that makes it difficult to tell where one stops and the other starts. If you don't know Grabiński, you're in for a treat. If you do know Grabiński, this book still reveals unexpected facets of his work. I hope you enjoy it as much as I do.

BRIAN EVENSON

A Night's Lodging

On my way back from visiting relatives, I had the unfortunate idea of covering the mile-long distance to the nearest railway station not by car, but on foot. It was the full bloom of a summer evening that enticed me, the chance to wander among fields of ripened wheat and meadows exuding scents of field herbs and flowers. But I had hardly made it halfway to the station when I began to regret my decision. The air became dense and humid; the clouds, previously scattered throughout the day, suddenly clustered into a threatening mass that hovered gloomily in the middle of the sky. A thunderstorm was brewing.

I hastened to reach the station before the eruption of the elements, simplifying my route by cutting through the woods. After a quarter-hour's hard walking on winding paths, I realized that my efforts were futile, and that I would not escape the storm. The mourning jacket of clouds was torn asunder by a blinding zigzag of lightning, and dull thuds began to disturb the forest calm. A heavy rain fell.

I took shelter from the first attack of this downpour beneath a hazel bush in a small lane packed with trees, waiting for the right moment.

Once the rain lightened, I left my hiding place and moved on. The soggy ground made it even harder to walk, and more than once I stumbled and nearly tripped over some fallen branch. To make matters worse, it was getting dark, and I was poorly acquainted with the area's labyrinthine paths and byways. After walking for another half hour, soaked halfway through with rain and wearied by my search for some road to salvation, I came to the sad realization that I had been heading entirely in the wrong direction and gotten myself lost in the forest.

It was a dreadful situation to be in. I lit a match so I could check my watch, which showed that it was already seven o'clock in the evening, far too late to catch any train. Although it had stopped raining, the prospect of spending the night in the woods on the damp ground did not appeal to me. With the instinct of a drowning man, I flung myself headlong down one particular path, looking neither right nor left, and breaking into a run between two rows of crooked pines.

Being in motion warmed me up and redoubled my strength; within about ten minutes a clearing came into view, and a moment later I emerged from the accursed forest into an open field stretching as far as the eye could see. I was on some kind of rutted path which, deeply embedded like a ravine between two large crop fields, glimmered in the darkening distance. I decided to follow it wherever it might lead, hoping to end up at some village or hamlet.

The moon, which had peeked out briefly from behind the clouds, concealed itself again in their thick folds, and I carried on in darkness.

It began to drizzle again, small, prickly drops that seemed to pierce straight through to the bone. I was freezing, wearing no overcoat and only light day-clothes. I continued to walk in total darkness, occasionally sticking out my hands to feel along the sides of the ravine for fear that I would stray from my course. Once I ended up in some kind of pit and had just managed to extricate myself from its sloshy, rain-soaked depths when I stumbled into a puddle of mud reaching up to my knees.

I kept walking. Gradually the ground rose, and the ravine became level with the surrounding fields. Beneath my feet I could feel an overgrown furrow forming the gap between two railroad tracks.

After a while, I picked up the scent of bird cherries somewhere to my right. I quickened my pace, taking in this smell with delight; it became stronger, intermingled with the aroma of acacia. Undoubtedly I was approaching some village or manor house. I heard rustling in the trees spread out above me, a grand and solemn conversation. I strained my eyes in the direction of the sound but could see nothing; the dark was absolute, black as a funeral shroud . . .

A wet branch brushed against my face, showering me in a cascade of droplets. I wiped my eyes and reached up to grab hold of it, but felt instead the stiff wood of a picket fence.

'An orchard,' I thought happily. 'Or a manor park. Either way, I'll have some shelter for the night.'

So as not to lose contact with it, I slid my fingers along the length of the spans as I advanced, as if along a thread guiding me through the darkness. At a certain point the fence gave way, tilting inward. A gate. I went in and closed it behind me, the squeal of its rusty hinges piercing the silence.

I walked along a narrow avenue shrouded by the swaying of trees which grew along either side; all around me was the rustling of leaves and the rattling of branches tossed about in the wind. I could see nothing – even the trunks of the unseen trees merged wholly into the blackness of night, with not a single detail to be distinguished. Having thus walked a few hundred steps, I suddenly bumped my head on something hard; reaching up to touch the obstacle, I found that it was the fencing. So here was where the garden ended; evidently the path I had taken was not the main one, but ran lengthwise across the property. The manor or farmhouse I supposed to exist must lay at the end of the main path, which at some point probably crossed the one I had taken at random. I had to find this point of intersection.

I turned around and started back carefully in the direction I had come, straying every few steps slightly to the left and to the right in hopes of finding the turn. Try as I might, however, I could not find the path which I imagined would lead me to the residence. Not daring to plunge off into the brush, where I might be stuck wandering until morning, I returned after each divergence to the middle of the path so as to feel out the terrain on the opposite side. I searched in vain, however, and after about fifteen minutes found myself back at the gate. Despairing at my failure, soaked to the gills, I resumed my efforts, this time sticking to the right side and examining it as thoroughly as possible.

I had gone only a few steps when I tripped over some protruding stump, instinctively reaching out to grab hold of the nearest tree. Instead of a trunk, my palm landed on what felt like the corner of a building. I stopped, running my hand along the wall. It was made of wood, rough planks of unpolished lumber. I felt the outlines of a door, latched shut with a wooden peg . . .

I hesitated: should I enter, or keep looking?

Surely this shack couldn't be a manor house?

My immense weariness settled the matter. I felt in that moment that I could not go on any further. Feeling myself begin to shiver with fever, I knocked on the door. There was no response from within. I pressed my ear to the wall, listening. Complete silence. Losing patience, I undid the latch and pushed against the door with all my strength. It opened without resistance.

I detected the smell of fresh hay and snuffed candles.

A peculiar combination, I thought, closing the door swiftly behind me.

'Good evening!' I called out.

'Good evening!' returned the echo.

The space I had entered was apparently empty. My voice resounded as though inside a barrel.

I attempted to strike one match, then another – unfortunately they would not comply, being just as soaked through as myself. I'd have to give up any hope of having light. I moved around the room, feeling my way blindly along the walls. Along the second one I was stopped by some object sticking out of a recess, which gave a dull thud when my foot struck it. I wanted to pass it and continue on, but my hand met empty space and I fell into some interior cavity. The object was apparently hollowed out.

What the hell?, I thought, clinging to the protruding edge. Some kind of wooden trough?

With some effort, I managed to get out of the thing. Suddenly I felt uneasy.

'Where am I?' I shouted at the top of my lungs.

Silence. I stood, straining to catch any sound in that deathly quiet. Not even the slightest exhalation of human breath disturbed the stillness of the night. I could hear nothing but my own quickening heartbeat . . .

I began to wander about the room. After a moment, my feet became tangled in what seemed to be scarves, or pieces of clothing discarded on the floor. I bent and picked one up. It was a damp, tattered rag, stinking of rot and old tallow candles. I tossed it away in disgust.

My weary brain speculated on the function of this place. Maybe a gardener's shed, or a disused apiary? The alluring scent of hay drew me towards the center of the room.

Perhaps I could sleep on it, even if on the floor?

I suddenly encountered an obstacle at about chest height: some kind of table or bunk, covered in a layer of fresh hay. I extended my hand and ran it with pleasure over the fragrant bedding. It was unoccupied; at last, I had found myself a bed.

Without a second thought, I threw off my soaked shirt, lay down my head, and stretched myself out delightfully on the bunk.

Outside the rain was still falling, drumming against the roof in large, heavy drops, and the wind was wailing in the trees. Lulled by the monotonous sounds of the elements, exhausted from a long tramp through the rain and thunder, I soon slipped into a hypnagogic state. For a short time I remained suspended in this space between waking and sleep, full of jumbled images, shapes and figures – until a thick, coagulated fog set in, stifling them with a blind veil. Finally the first wave of sleep washed over me, plunging me into its depths. Soon, carried off by this mysterious current, I found myself somewhere far away, in completely new and unfamiliar surroundings, among strangers in elegant dress . . .

The interior of an old-fashioned manor house. On the walls, Turkish tapestries, ancestral portraits, a hunting rifle. A large, bright room, clouded with tobacco smoke. At the center, around a table covered in green cloth, a group of men in evening clothes. They are playing cards: whist. Their faces are tired, rumpled, no doubt from a sleepless night. The focus shifts onto three figures – two men and a woman. Beautiful people, particularly the blond man with his characteristic English profile. A purebred fellow. He plays nervously, distractedly, frequently losing. Every now and then, dark violet eyes look up from the cards and stare at the pale, black-haired woman in a scarlet shawl sitting beside the other man, presumably her husband.

There is something that binds these two together, a strong, heartfelt secret. The woman's gaze never strays from the blond man's face — she sucks in the sweetness of his love-drunk eyes. The husband's face is focused, marble-like, a deep furrow etched across his brow beneath a head of abundant, chestnut-colored hair. He plays evenly, calmly, only from time to time leaning over toward the dying candle at his right to light a cigarette from its flame. Then, for an instant, his steel-gray eyes seek out those of his opponent and fix upon them coldly, with intense attention . . . The game goes on in its inexorable, fatal course.

Time draws on in long seconds, minutes, hours . . . Suddenly, the lady subtly withdraws her round, wonderfully sculpted arm from under the shawl and seeks the hand of her lover. Their hands meet in the blink of an eye, for a brief, divine instant and, frightened, draw back again.

The husband quivers uneasily, forcefully suppressing a tremor of his already-raised hand. Only his face turns gray as ash and wrinkles in irritation, until by an effort of will he smooths it into a mask of indifference. He has noticed . . .

The blond man begins dealing cards. Kings, jacks, an ace of diamonds that whirls in midair and falls upon the cloth . . .

The woman gets up and says something. She apologizes to the guests and orders a morning refreshment be served. Passing by the blond man, she grazes against his cheek lightly, as if by accident, with the wide sleeve of her kimono. Her full, robust, yet supple figure disappears behind a portière into an adjoining room. The men give her a parting nod and resume playing.

Evidently the hand in progress is very interesting, as for a moment the faces become animated and everyone's attention is fully focused. The master of the house has won . . .

A maidservant enters with a tray, offering tea and pastries. The guests begin breakfasting. The servant takes advantage of the commotion and the chairs being pushed back to slip a small, rolled-up note into the blond man's hand. He clutches it hastily, taking a quick glance around, then relaxes, exhaling: no one has seen . . .

Noticing the lady's absence, her husband asks the servant something and leaves the room. A perfect opportunity. The happy rival absconds over to a window frame, unrolls the paper, and reads it. A wave of blood reddens his cheeks, lights dance in his eyes. He rolls it up, slides it into his breast pocket . . . Then, finishing his cigarette, he moves back into the room and disappears amid the bustle through the door opposite the portière.

After a while, the husband returns. His face shows agitation, a flash of anger. There has been an argument. A fat gentleman pulls him to a corner of the room for a private chat. He allows himself to be led, although grudgingly. Fifteen minutes pass, then half an hour.

The dispersed guests gradually return to their seats around the green table. The blond man's absence is noted. Smiles break out across some faces; hinting remarks are made, insinuations. Subtle glances center upon the master of the house.

He rises from his chair, pale, tremulous.

'Please excuse me, gentlemen. I am obliged to locate our missing guest. I shan't be long.'

He throws the curtain aside and enters the main quarters of the house. A long row of rooms can be seen, old chambers muffled by damask curtains, stretching all the way to the garden on the other side of the house. One set of doors is opened, another, panels anxiously flung aside, heavy curtains drawn back . . . Malicious probing eyes scan corners, drill into alcoves, inspect the bedroom . . .

Exiting onto the porch, he descends the stairs and turns left along the footpath. His steps are quiet, careful, stealthy. Voices can be heard, passionate whispers. He looks through the lattice of wild vines into the bower. He watches . . . her head resting upon his breast, she offers him her lips. A long, protracted kiss . . .

Suddenly, the scene changes. The husband is standing in the center of the bower, a cold, ironic smile on his lips, and a riding crop in his hand.

'*Excusez!*'

The woman jumps up from the bench and is about to say something, but he cuts her off with a swish of the cane. Letting out a short cry, she raises her hand to her cheek, where an elongated, reddish-blue welt has formed . . . The man rushes forward in a rage, raising his hand to strike her. But he meets resistance: an arm, strong as steel, stops him in his course.

'We'll have to find another way to settle this matter.'

With an imperious motion, he extends his hand toward the woman and points to the house.

'Please leave us alone!'

She walks away. A silent game of faces, a duel of stares. The rivals' eyes, locked together in a death-grip, almost simultaneously fall upon a knitting basket which the lady had left on the table. Two balls of yarn inside stick out noticeably: one green, one blue. The husband's lips contort into a strange smile. He picks them up, rolls them around in his palms. Then, looking inquiringly at the other man, he holds up the blue ball.

'Death.'

Then, the green one.

'Life.'

'All right.'

'Who will draw the lots?'

Their exchange is interrupted by a large English greyhound. The handsome creature trots into the bower with quick, lithe steps and begins to fawn at the feet of the blond man, who strokes the dog's head. Then, gesturing at the dog:

'Nero.'

'Fine.'

The husband places the two balls back into the basket on the table. His rival in turn removes them and, taking both in his right hand, says to the dog:

'*Apporte*, Nero! *Apporte!*'

The colored balls fly from his hands and, tracing a double parabola, land a few dozen steps down the path. The green one comes to rest nearest them, with the blue a few meters behind it.

'*Apporte*, Nero!' urges the blond man again.

Nero darts out and slows to a light trot as he approaches the balls. Both men watch his movements carefully from the bower. He takes the green one in his jaws, and is just about to return to his master with the prize when he notices the blue one just behind him, beside a flower bed. He hesitates for a moment, uncertain how to proceed; then he trots over to the flower bed and picks up that one also. Proud of having conscientiously resolved the prob- lem, he begins heading back to the bower, holding both balls in his upraised snout. Suddenly, one of his paws becomes caught on a root and, jolting up to free himself, he swipes his head against a bush; one of the balls slips from his jaws and rolls beneath the shrubs. A moment later, panting, he drops the remaining ball at his master's feet: the blue ball of death.

The blond man picks it up, stroking the dog's lustrous, silky coat:

'Thank you, Nero.'

He smiles and, regarding the victor, adds calmly:

'A valiant beast. Yes, yes. My own dog. I bid you farewell, sir.'

The latter responds with a silent bow.

With a quick, nervous step he leaves the bower, crosses the park and goes out the gate to the fields. Nero runs after him. The young man slows his step and turns into the willow thicket running behind the manor house. He walks along the riverbank, overgrown with calamus and bulrushes, mechanically brushing aside the dew- covered shoots as he plunges into a forest of wet rime. Among the greenery, drenched in the gold of the morning sun, the black con- tours of his slender, well-cut tailcoat stand out boldly.

The dog accompanies him all the while, following in his tracks, though the man seems not to notice him. Suddenly, having emerged from the thicket into a small meadow, he turns and regards his faithful companion. Anger flashes in his despair-glazed eyes. He runs up and kicks the dog with all his might.

'Go away, you vile beast!'

The dog yelps, staggers, looks reproachfully into his master's eyes. The latter turns and continues on, straying again toward the river. His dull gaze wanders over the waves, is carried along on the current's flow. At his feet, the dog whimpers meekly, apologizing for his unknown offense, licking at his hands, fawning against him. The man removes a small snub-nosed revolver from his pocket and shoots him in the head. The animal lets out a low groan and falls at his master's feet, shattered skull coming to rest upon its out- stretched paws.

Deep in despair, and recognizing the gun to be now empty, he tosses it into the reeds as something unnecessary. Then, with no further thought, he jumps into the river. The water beneath him churns, swells, sends up a splash of foam, then closes over its victim in a smooth, even sheet. Currents flow on toward distant shores, waves tumble and roll out their itinerant fate, the river rushes forth in its errant course with the longing of the eternal wanderer . . .

And all is quiet at the river's edge; quiet, and lonely. Here, a mottled blue roller rattles in the thicket, a gnat buzzes, a frog croaks – there, a gadwall zigzags overhead, a diaphanous dragon-fly hesitates over a coltsfoot leaf . . . Occasionally there sounds a duck's frightened response call, a wild goose's whooping, a tern's whine. In the distance, at the bend where the ribbon of water disappears among the thickets, a drowsy fog slumbers . . .

Slowly, wreaths of mist extend from there across the landscape; dark veils enshroud the river, loop around ice floes, obscure the banks – until everything merges into one great, formless, grayish-white cloud . . .

Suddenly, a red blast of light struck my eyes, and I woke up. It was a fine, bright day. I was lying on my back, my face exposed to the sun's rays streaming in through a small grated window in the opposite wall. Blinded by the glare, I shielded my eyes and inspected my surroundings. An unpleasant shock ran through my body. There was a coffin in the corner, its exposed interior radiating with the void of death . . .

I averted my eyes, which then fell upon the protruding corner of the bunk I was lying upon. It was covered with some black cloth, or a piece of some tattered material. I took it in my hand; it was the ragged old shroud-cloth, begrimed with dust and mud, spattered with wax drippings. I remembered the previous night, and the rag I had picked up in the darkness. Brrr . . . I kicked it off the bunk with my foot.

I rubbed my eyes. All of my drowsiness had gone. I was fully returned to my senses.

Where was I?

Under my left hand, beneath the hay bedding, I felt some hard object which I had been involuntarily grasping with my fingers.

Laziness deterred me from getting up and figuring out what it was; I only turned my head to see a layered wall of straw and hay which covered my hand, and whatever it was holding. I began to run my fingers along the length of it. How peculiar! I now had the impression that I was touching something soft, made of cloth, like ... someone's sleeve. At once, I understood. All night long, I had been inadvertently holding on to the arm of a man. In one motion, I flung myself off the bunk, turned and sat down. The mound of straw partially collapsed, revealing the body of a man lying beside me on the other half of the bunk. A quick glance at his face froze the blood in my veins: it was the blond man I had seen in the dream.

It was the same aristocratic face, the same refined features, but now more sharply accentuated by death's stylus. He was lying stiffly on the straw bedding in a damp, rumpled tailcoat with clumps of aquatic plants like pendants in his thick, bright hair and streaks of mud on his pants and shirt-front.

I stared at him, dumbstruck, not believing my eyes.

Abruptly, I jumped off the corpse's bed and, not looking back, began putting on my shirt. I wanted to get out of there as fast as I could, and go as far away as I could.

Suddenly, I heard the sound of voices and people walking outside. The door swung open and several men walked in: three peasants led by the mayor, a policeman, a sickly-looking man who looked like a clerk, and two gentlemen. The group had a solemn, official bearing. A commission of inquiry, I thought.

'What are you doing here?' asked the mayor in a gruff voice.

'What of it? I had to spend the night here.'

'That's not allowed. This is a mortuary,' he rebuked harshly.

'I ended up here last night while trying to escape the rain. I didn't know what kind of place this was.'

'Congratulations on your night's lodging,' said one of the gentlemen, a lanky dark-haired man with a goatee, probably a doctor.

'Indeed, I had something of a strange sleep. This body ... ?'

'Some of the locals pulled it out of the water yesterday afternoon. It had washed up on the riverbank, near the mill.'

'I presume, gentlemen, that you're here to begin the autopsy?' I asked.

'That's right. The commission is all here. Judge,' he turned to a stout man in a clerk's cap with a briefcase under his arm. 'Shall we wait for Mr. Giżycki's arrival?'

'Here is his Honorable Lordship, the squire himself,' answered the peasants in a chorus, making room for the man just now crossing the threshold of the mortuary.

He removed his large white Panama hat and, taking a quick glance at the bier, turned white as a sheet. I recognized him as the husband from my dream. There was a deep silence. The doctor opened a large walnut case and began laying out his postmortem examination tools. The cold blades of his lancets glinted in the light, the metallic clatter of knives and tweezers filled the room.

It was then that I gave a silent bow to all present and made my way out the front door.

Outside, I was greeted by a cemetery bathed in morning dew, resounding with the chatter of insects and birds. I walked along a white sand path with rows of graves on either side. Crooked crosses jutted out from among the bird-cherry thickets, wearing necklaces of withered wreaths; a blackened Madonna statuette leaned from behind a bouquet of jasmine; sepulchral angels extended their dislocated wings ... Tears of rain pearled in the graveyard grass and made rainbows of the sunlight. Moist, warm air exuded from the waterlogged earth, soaked up the scents of flowers and herbs and wafted them up over the trees. On a weeping birch by the gate, a skittish gray bird sat, mewling faintly ...

At Sarah's House

At the most recent club meeting, I was much appalled by Stosławski's attitude and behavior. This usually cheerful and open fellow had changed beyond recognition. He hardly took part in the discussion, and when he did, made statements irrelevant to the topic, confounding those present; I even noticed some ironic glances directed at my unfortunate colleague by the more spiteful among us. I tried to defend him by connecting the words he had flung out with the conversation at hand – then he smiled feebly, as if thankful for my rescue, and remained obstinately silent until the end.

Generally speaking, he made a very negative impression on me at that time. Not only was I vexed by his unusual reticence, so at odds with his prior disposition, but also by his puzzling appearance. Usually well groomed, even excessively stylish, Stosławski showed up that evening looking unkempt, almost decrepit. His face, once healthy and vibrant with the glow of youth, had gone deathly pale, his eyes cast over by a fog of distraction, their dull inertia forming a painful contrast with the noble contours of his features.

Struck by a sense of foreboding, I invited him to come round after the session and subjected him to a careful medical examination. He made no objection, although it was already late, and patiently allowed himself to be examined. Apart from considerable nervous exhaustion and general weakness, I found nothing unusual. I only wondered about the cause.

'Hey, Kazio!' I joked, wagging a finger at him. 'You're having too much fun! Women, eh? Too much, my friend, too much! You have to take better care of yourself. You can't carry on like this. You'll run yourself ragged soon enough. And then what?'

I had struck the right chord.

'Women . . .' he remarked thoughtfully, 'women . . . Why do you speak of many, and not just one?'

'If I know you, my dear friend,' I answered, smiling, 'none of them has yet succeeded in snaring you, spoiled favorite of the fairer sex. Have you really changed so suddenly? It's hard to imagine that you could be in love.'

'You've used the wrong expression just now. Do you not conceive of any other possibility besides love or transient lust?'

'What do you have in mind?'

'Sexual possession. Do you understand me?'

'Not exactly.'

'Well, it's very simple. One fine day you meet an exceptional woman, the very epitome of the female sex, and from that moment on, once you've been to bed with her, you cannot part with her. You hate her, you want to cast off the shackles, but your efforts are futile. You are utterly possessed by her sexual presence; your entire mental horizon is exclusively limited to her body, her curves, her looks, her touch; physical contact with her becomes a mode of existence. The woman turns into an idol, evil and despised, but nevertheless alluring, to which you must submit unconditionally . . .'

'That's just the heightened libido of a man who's found his type.'

'No, you're wrong; it's a kind of continuous, waking hypnotic suggestion. I simply cannot think about anything else but her and, most appallingly, her sexuality and anything related to it. I feel that this is being forced upon me against my will and even my libido; I have had women more beautiful and attractive than her, and yet I walked away with a light heart, breaking things off without hesitation. In this case, I don't have the strength to resist.'

'Evidently none of those others had met all of the conditions for your ideal woman.'

'That's not it. It seems to me – no, rather, I know for certain – that if I had not been intimate with her, I would not have ended up in this state. Would you believe this came about from a kind of seduction on her part?'

'Ha, ha! This is too much! Kazio Stosławski, a man pure of heart! That's what I call sexual refinement!'

'No, Władek! You're not trying to understand me. I didn't want to get too close to her due to a vague fear. I had a strange feeling.'

'But ultimately you gave in?'

'Unfortunately. I could not refuse. She's a beautiful woman, after all, and seemed to me at the time to be *une femme charmante* in the fullest sense of the word.'

'So you did not pursue her with any more eagerness than you did the others?'

'Certainly not. I only complied with her ardent wish, with a certain amount of resistance and apprehension.'

'And so . . . after the first time, she had you spellbound? You must have experienced sensations you'd never felt before?'

'No, indeed. I know them all by heart. I'm no novice, and sophistication is commonplace for me. She was even more subdued than the others.'

'So then, how is it that this woman has possessed you?'

'I don't know, I really have no idea. But right after that horrible tryst, I understood that I had fallen under her absolute control, that I had become a plaything in the hands of a demonic female. She knew that after our first intercourse I would become her prey, and that no one could tear me away from her. A peculiar bond had formed between us, like an elusive yet powerful chain, wrapping and constricting me ever more tightly . . .'

'Is she physically abusing you? You look much the worse for wear . . .'

'I can't complain too much about that. She weakens me, I feel it quite distinctly, drains me slowly, systematically, inexorably – but not through frequent intercourse . . .'

'I don't understand . . .'

'I just can't fathom how she does it. But there's no doubt that she is responsible for the strange condition you see me in. This woman is robbing me of all my vital powers with the rapacity of a vampire – do you get what I'm saying, Władek? She's absorbing my life, my youth, cruelly and relentlessly . . .'

'Put a stop to it. Can't you summon up some manly resolve?'

'I can't, I can't. I'm powerless. I've moved in with her, you know; we've been living together for two years in her villa outside the city, in Polanka.'

'Ah, now I understand why it's been so long since I've seen you out on the street, or at the café or theater. Does she forbid you to go out?'

'Not at all – I have no desire to do so myself. I did not avoid the company of people at first, but over time I began to limit myself to having contact exclusively with her. I no longer feel the need to exchange ideas with people with whom I have nothing in common. I only ended up at the club by chance today. I'm doing nothing with myself, I've become utterly apathetic toward everything ... My attitude toward the world is gradually unraveling! I'm spinning off in some kind of centrifugal direction, as though hovering between heaven and earth. I am still aware of it now, but who knows what will happen tomorrow ...'

I looked at him intently, with deep compassion.

'You're not well, Kazio,' I said, breaking the prolonged silence. 'You need treatment. Your nerves are out of whack. Maybe you are unjustly accusing her of exerting a negative influence; maybe the germs of the sickness were already within you when you made her acquaintance?'

He shook his head:

'No, my mind's quite made up on the matter. I noticed the symptoms in myself after we had been living together for a year. Besides, this is no nervous disorder. There's something else involved here, something our psychiatrists have never even dreamed of.'

'Perhaps. But who is this demon, this vampire in female form? Can you tell me her name?'

'Her name is Sarah Braga ...'

'Sarah Braga ... strange name! Is she Jewish? The name makes me think of the Old Testament.'

'No. Supposedly she's Protestant. The family has died out. From the few things she's told me, I suspect that the blood of the old Cortes of Castile flows in her veins, later mixed with a Germanic element; she represents a singular kind of cross-breeding.

It's been difficult for me to find out anything more because she doesn't like to talk about herself and her past. She was widowed years ago. Who her husband was, I do not know; she bears the name of her own family.'

'Do you know her age?'

'She maintains that she's in her thirties, although at first glance she looks younger. It's hard to be certain. She doesn't use any artificial means to enhance her outward appearance; in fact, she has an intense loathing for cosmetics of any sort. Having lived so intimately with her, I know this perfectly well ... Would you believe that there are strange rumors circulating about her and her age? From a few casual allusions and offhand remarks the servants have let slip, I've come to believe that Sarah is much older than she appears. She is a thoroughly enigmatic woman. The house is pervaded with a sense of mystery, a mystery dark and evil, like its occupant.'

He ran his hand across his forehead wearily:

'You've tired me out, Władek, forcing me to focus like this. I've got a fierce headache. Goodbye.'

'I'm sorry, but I did it out of friendship. I was alarmed by your appearance. I can relieve the pain easily, just stay a moment longer. I'll put you to sleep for five minutes and remove the pain by suggestion. How does that sound?'

'All right. Just don't keep me any longer.'

I got to work immediately. Being a skilled hypnotist, within two minutes I had him in a deep sleep ... As I was giving the suggestion against the headache, a thought suddenly occurred to me. Knowing that I would find it difficult to persuade him to visit me or the club again while in his normal state, I told him in his sleep to visit me the next month at the same time. It would be impossible for me to see him sooner, as I had at that time an intensive work schedule and was frequently out of town. Having given both orders, I made a few quick *passes contraires* and Stosławski awoke.

'Well, how do you feel now?' I asked.

'The pain's totally gone. Thank you. I've got to be off now. Farewell!'

'Or rather: see you later! When will you come around again?'

'I don't know; perhaps never. I cannot promise anything.'

He gave my hand a firm shake and departed.

When his footsteps had died away down the corridor, I returned to the living room, where clouds of smoke from our cigarettes still hung in the air. I sat down by the fireplace and, mechanically stroking the shiny coat of my faithful Astor, fell into a reverie.

'Sarah Braga! Sarah Braga! ... I've encountered that name once before in my life, although I don't know the person. Sarah Braga ... Yes! ...' I recalled it now, though vaguely; I'd read it in a list of patients of my former master, Dr. Żmuda, professor of neurology, some dozen years ago. I was still a young student of medicine then. Fortunately, I had kept a copy of the register, which was valuable because, in addition to the patients' names, it contained their diagnoses and the treatment methods for their diseases. 'I need to find it and take a look through it. Maybe I will learn more details.'

I opened the door of the bookcase and began to flip through the thick folio. I went back a number of years, not really trusting my memory. Suddenly I landed upon the entry, which was dated July, 1875, and read as follows:

'Sarah Braga, resident of the villa "Tofana" in Polanka, born in 1830, age 45 – body exceptionally resistant to signs of aging – psychopathic tendencies linked to sexuality – symptoms of psychological sadism.'

This was followed by abbreviated notes regarding recommended therapies and treatments.

'So, she would be around eighty years old today! Phenomenal! Unbelievable! ... Stosławski maintains that she is young and beautiful! Could it be someone else? But the address strangely coincides. Villa Tofana in Polanka, a suburban district; a kind of summer resort in the capital – how odd! But what does all this have to do with Kazio's condition? What he said was too vague and subjective for me to draw any conclusions. I suppose time will tell.'

The following day I was forced to leave town unexpectedly on business. I was so engrossed in my work that I almost forgot about Stosławski's story. It was only when I finally returned to the city after a month's absence that I recalled that the following day was the deadline for fulfillment of my hypnotic command. And indeed, around four o'clock in the afternoon, Stosławski walked mechanically into my living room.

I had him sit, put him to sleep again and, having praised him for the conscientious fulfillment of the task, woke him up.

When he came to, he looked around the room in astonishment, unsure how he had gotten there. When I explained the situation he calmed down a bit, but a look of resentment and displeasure emanated from his face. His transformation had progressed frightfully in the past month, and it was apparent that he was moving at a disastrous speed in a mysterious direction.

I hastily and deliberately began to converse about trivial things, wholly unrelated to his unusual condition, and avoided asking about his relationship with Sarah. He answered apathetically and with difficulty, often breaking the thread of the conversation with meaningless interjections of no apparent relevance.

It didn't take long to recognize that he had become detached from reality and had almost completely lost his sense of time and space. Likewise, his sense of perspective with regard to events and objects, of their variations in dimension and degree, had ceased to exist: everything lay on one ideal plane. Past events took on the dramatic form of the present moment, the mystery of the future intruded so thoroughly upon the immediate present as to be wholly indistinguishable from it. The three-dimensionality of things had been irretrievably lost, giving way to a kind of paradoxical single-planarity.

Pale and bloodless, his face peered out at the world like a mask, indifferent to its affairs, the complexity of which seemed to have disappeared under the pressure of a mysterious kind of simplification. His hand, raised in alabaster whiteness, almost transparent, made a gesture of eternal duration, as if symbolic of something essential and unchanged from the earliest ages of being . . .

He had become inert, moving slowly, lazily, as if in a dream. He allowed me to examine him with indifference. I subjected him to X-rays; the light quickly passed through him, encountering abnormally reduced resistance. The results were far beyond anything I'd ever witnessed: his body had undergone an alarming depletion; the skeletal system showed signs of atrophy, whole masses of tissue had disappeared, clusters of cells degenerated. He was as light as a child; the iron fingers of the scale indicated a ridiculously low number. This man was disappearing before my eyes!

I wanted to keep him with me and, if at all possible, prevent his complete deterioration. I thought that his passivity would make my task easier, and that he would not resist me, but I was mistaken. After a two-hour conversation he suddenly rose like an automaton and began to take his leave. He was compelled to head home, to the villa Tofana. It seemed that, with all of his interests in life having faded away, all that was left was this elemental, unstoppable urge to go to her, to Sarah, towards whom he was drawn with the whole of his enfeebled personality. It was difficult to oppose. I felt that if I did not let him go, something bad would happen: his eyes were already flickering with the fires of an unsettled and dangerous force . . .

So I decided to take him to the place in a droshky. Polanka was quite far from the center of town, and it was only after a half-hour ride that we reached our destination.

I helped him out and guided him toward the marble staircase leading to the villa. At the door to the sunroom I hesitated, uncertain whether to go inside with him or turn back. Suddenly, I was overcome with an overwhelming desire to meet this woman. But I did not dare to go on further. Of course, I was completely at ease with Stosławski – he didn't seem to mind my presence at all – but the behavior of the footman who hurried out to greet us had an inhibiting effect. This clean-shaven lackey in his impeccable tailcoat greeted my companion with a deep bow, but a smile of flippant irony played on his face; he looked upon me as an intruder who should be turned out at once.

I was just about to return to my waiting carriage when the velvet curtains separating the veranda from the interior of the house suddenly parted and a woman stepped out before their orange background.

To call her 'beautiful' would be to capture her surface appearance from an essentially false point of view. She was instead demonically, even devilishly, alluring. Her irregular features, wide, fleshy lips, and strongly developed nose did not give the impression of beauty – and yet the face, with its dazzlingly white, matte complexion, contrasting all the more strongly with the fiery gaze of her burning black eyes, bound the observer with an indescribable force. She had a kind of elemental simplicity which, confident in its power, despises accessories.

Her raven hair washed over her immaculate, beautifully curved forehead in gentle waves and was fastened at the summit of her royal head by a silver headband. Her dark green, elegantly cut damask gown flowed smoothly along her haughty figure, accentuating the exquisite lines of her torso and supple, virginally compact hips.

I glared fiercely into her bewitching, hellish eyes, focusing the whole of my will into the stare. She responded, parrying the attack. We struggled against each other for a moment. Then her face showed hesitation, uncertainty, fear; she shuddered with discomfort. I made a deep bow, took hold of Stosławski's hand and said:

'I am escorting this fugitive home, commending him to your loving care.'

And I told her my name.

Sarah gave a nod of her head and, pulling back the curtain, invited us inside; she did not pay the slightest attention to Stosławski, who watched her all the while as though hypnotized. He was sad to look at. His eyes were trained on her with unquestioning, canine humility, a kind of servile obedience. At the sound of her voice, he hurried towards her as though seeking support, to be cared for; the woman smiled half contemptuously, half graciously and, stopping him with a careless wave of her hand, turned to give orders to the footman, who was watching the scene with indifference:

'Bring the master to his bedroom; he is weary, he must rest.'

Without a word, the servant lifted him from under his arms and almost dragged him in through the side door.

I followed Sarah into the living room.

It was stylish, with high vaulted ceilings and everything upholstered in a soft, silky fabric the color of terracotta. There were no windows; the living room was lit by a massive chandelier hanging from the center of the ceiling.

The front half of the room was nearly empty; along the walls ran two rows of chairs with pearl inlay on their backs and armrests. Exotic shrubs in large silver urns jutted out from niches between them.

Further into the room a podium rose up several steps, covered in cloth of a luscious shade of cinnabar. A vase of flowers sat on the table at the center of the stage, which was draped in a heavy coverlet adorned with beryl pendants. A pair of tabourets, an Eastern ottoman, and a slender rosewood piano filled the rest of the space.

A curtain similar to the one at the entrance formed the back wall, its rippling fabric closing off the unseen interior.

I trod quietly, my feet sinking into the lush fur of the carpets spread across the floor. The lady led me to the podium and, indicating one of the chairs, lowered herself carelessly onto the ottoman.

I sat down silently. After a moment, Sarah reached for the box of cigarettes on a small table nearby. Having noticed that the table was a bit out of her reach, I pushed it closer to the sofa and then handed her a burning match.

'Thank you.' She inhaled the smoke. 'You don't smoke?'

'Yes . . .' I took out a cigar from the adjacent compartment and, puffing out a purple cloud, remarked with appreciation: 'Fabulous!'

'You bore me. Is this how you usually entertain women?'

'It depends on their type. With a lady such as yourself, for example, I find it difficult to talk; it is easy to strike a false tone. I have to get comfortable with you.'

Sarah looked into my eyes, trying to put on a look of silken softness. It was then that I noticed a striking resemblance to Stosławski in her features. She looked surprised:

'What's the matter? You look like someone who has just made a great discovery.'

'Indeed, I have discovered something peculiar.'

She drew herself up with a sneer. 'What is it, please? . . . Can you tell me?'

'You are strangely similar to Kazio.'

Sarah's face twitched:

'An illusion.'

'No, ma'am. I'm a pretty good physiognomist. In any case, it can be explained: You have been living together for a long time . . . Such close cohabitation makes each more resemble the other.'

'Hm . . . Is that your theory?'

'No, my dear lady – this theory, not a new one by any means, was discussed in great detail a few years ago by Dr. Żmuda.'

I lied in attributing this alleged theory to Żmuda, only wanting to introduce his name into the conversation.

'Dr. Żmuda?' she asked curiously. 'Are you perhaps his student?'

'Not at all,' I denied vigorously. 'I don't even know him. I've only read an essay of his in a medical magazine.'

'Oh, I see . . .'

'Are you acquainted with him?'

'Yes. I was a patient of his last year, suffering from a slight nervous disorder. A very nice man.'

'So, she is the same woman,' I thought, 'only she had the treatment much earlier, thirty-five years ago, in 1875. So this woman, blossoming with the charm of youth, would be eighty years old today! Extraordinary! Unbelievable! And yet it must be so; Żmuda's notes and my memory remove all doubt.'

I looked at Sarah with a vague disquiet.

'Why have you suddenly become so serious? One would think you are afraid of something?'

'This time the illusion is yours, truly, my lady. Why should I be afraid? I'm merely overwhelmed by your exceptional beauty. One rarely meets women such as yourself.'

She smiled with satisfaction.

'You horrid flatterer!'

She struck me gently on the shoulder. Although I am usually in full control of myself, I winced involuntarily under this touch, tilting my head up slightly. Then my gaze landed on a series of portraits hanging on the left wall of the room. I put down my cigar and walked over to the paintings.

There were ten of them in two parallel rows; the top row comprised five images of Sarah – below it were placed the likenesses of five men I did not know. Two striking details were immediately apparent. In all of the portraits, Sarah looked about the same age, as if they had been painted at short intervals from one another. Yet in each, the facial expression was different, and remarkably similar to that of the man in the row below it; in a word, each of the five likenesses of Sarah had its counterpart in the images of the men, in terms of outward resemblance.

Busy studying the images, I did not notice her displeasure. Only Sarah's voice, sharp and impatient, interrupted my observations:

'Will you finish up this review already? There's nothing interesting there – just cheap daubs!'

'On the contrary – exquisite works! What expressiveness of features! My dear lady has a truly sphinx-like face; it seems to be constantly changing, yet always the same. The men's faces, too, are superb – all pure-bred types! Cousins, maybe? Perhaps not? They do not resemble each other at all – each of their faces is different.'

'Friends,' she answered dryly. 'Please, come back here – closer to me,' she added more warmly, indicating the place beside her on the sofa.

I sat down, still preoccupied with the mystery of the men's faces, each of which vividly resembled Sarah's, although they were in no way related to one another.

Observing my thoughtfulness, she tried hard to distract me with conversation. Soon we strayed upon women's favorite topic and began to talk about love. Here, Sarah's tone at once became passionate, and she showed a predilection for discussing cases so extreme they bordered on degeneracy. She betrayed a most unusual knowledge of all the nuances of sexuality, in which perversion competed with lasciviousness. And she knew how to present everything in a sophisticated, strangely stylized and appealing manner; evidently she wanted to enchant me not only with her physical beauty, but also with the wealth of erotic possibilities that lay within her.

Recognizing this obvious intention, I was on my guard. An indefinite fear repulsed me from this woman and demanded caution. Still, so as not to discourage her by my coldness, I feigned excitement, returning her devilish gaze with my own fiery eyes.

Around ten o'clock in the evening I took my leave, promising to visit again soon.

However, my next visit was delayed longer than I had anticipated.

Summoned by telegraph to F., two days' journey away, I left the following day for an extended period, and it was three weeks before I had occasion to return to the Villa Tofana. Sarah ran out to greet me, radiant with joy. When I asked how Stosławski was, she grew somber and shrugged her shoulders dismissively:

'Boring.'

Concealing my indignation at her unbounded selfishness, I expressed my wish to see him. She acquiesced reluctantly, and only at my insistence:

'I cannot refuse you; but you must go into the bedroom, for he won't come out from there.'

And she led me through the living room into a quiet chamber furnished with a refined softness.

The sight of Stosławski made a terrifying impression on me. He stood staring vacantly out the window, picking at the tassels of the drapes with his right hand. He didn't recognize me, perhaps didn't even notice me.

A dull smile wandered across his face and his flaccid, paper-white lips moved weakly, forming words; he was whispering something. I moved in closer, listening carefully. His speech was barely audible, but I have a sharp ear and was able to make out the words. There were only a few of them, repeated incessantly as if by an automaton: the same shameless, cynical words of endearment . . .

There was something at once so hideous and monstrous in it that I had to back out of the room, trembling.

Here was a case beyond redemption. The man was lost.

Disturbed by this horrible sight, I departed immediately for home, despite Sarah's pleas.

I came to a firm decision. I strongly doubted the possibility of saving Stosłaski; the state into which he had fallen had taken on too extravagant a form even to dream of a reversion. All I could do was exact revenge – calm, deliberate, planned – because I was faced with no ordinary opponent.

I would have to arm myself with uncompromising coldness and resistance to the devilish charms of this woman, whose destructive hold probably only set in with the consummation of the sexual act. The words of my unfortunate friend, which I had previously disregarded, now rang in my ears:

'I feel as though if I'd not had any closer intercourse with her, I would not have ended up the way I am now.'

Whatever role Sarah's influence played in the matter, I had to be careful. She had already displayed an unambiguous attraction toward me and, for all I knew, could have already marked me as Stosławski's successor. I decided to take advantage of this, giving the appearance of willingness to agree to future propositions. But I had to wait; it was still too early to act.

In the meantime, I went to her house frequently, visiting at every free moment. But since the last scene in the bedroom, she had not once allowed me to see the sick man, no doubt fearing that my suspicions would discourage me. I gave in, contenting myself with amusements in the living room and reading together. So passed the days and weeks, during which I observed Sarah's passion for me grow ever more intense. But not once did I allow her to cross the bounds of social propriety, thus strengthening her depraved lust all the more. My self-restraint irritated her, fanned the flames. Gradually I became master of the situation . . .

One evening I arrived a little later than usual, around nine o'clock, to spend a bit of time together over dinner.

It was a pleasant day in June. A light evening breeze wafted through the open dining-room window, gently ruffling the lace of the curtains. The aroma of flowers drifted in from the park, thick with the scent of blooming jasmines. From amid the row of maples came the plaintive cries of nightingales and the occasional soft chirping of drowsy crickets.

I sat in an armchair with my legs extended, sipping coffee. Sarah was playing a dizzying Dervishes' dance on the piano. I watched her hands move violently, fanatically, as they struck out tones in a hot-blooded frenzy, impassioned, intoxicated. At that moment, she was beautiful. A deep flush had crept into her pale face, lightning flashed in her eyes, her quickened breath making her white negligee undulate like waves of foam over her wonderfully curved breast.

Right in the midst of the most heightened abandon, when I was listening to the piece and drinking in the heat of this exotic music, a thought about Stosławski hit me like a thunderbolt.

Where was he now, what was he doing? Still smiling as he had been then, wedged in the corner of the adjacent room? Or maybe Sarah's playing could galvanize even that shell of a human for just a moment? But then what? What groans of bottomless despair must wrack that remnant of a man!

I leapt up from my seat as if thrown from it and, pressing my hand on the keyboard, shouted:

'Enough! I want to see Stosławski! At once!'

Surprised, Sarah straightened up haughtily and sized me up with impassive eyes:

'You will not see him.'

'I must! Do you understand? I must! Today, right now! Or else I . . .'

But I did not finish my threat, because at that moment Sarah's robe was suffused with a scarlet glow, as though she stood in flames before me.

'What's that?' we cried in unison, forgetting all else.

Turning automatically toward the window, we saw the bloody glow of fire rising over the crowns of the trees in the park.

From elsewhere in the house we heard the din of confused voices and screams, muffled moments before by the music. A servant rushed into the dining room, pale with fear:

'My lady, Polanka is on fire! The gamekeeper's house is up in flames!'

Sarah looked questioningly at me.

'Please, go to my carriage. It's waiting at the front gate,' I decided hastily.

'And you?'

'I'll be right there, please wait in the carriage – we'll leave together. I have to save one of your portraits in the salon, the last, the best one . . .'

I led her out and, having instructed the servant to help her into the vehicle, went back alone into the villa. It wasn't the portrait I was concerned about, but Stosławski. I could not leave him at the mercy of the flames.

I burst open the bedroom door and rushed inside, calling:

'Kazio! It's me! There's a fire, come on! Get out of here!'

I was met with silence. The bedroom was dark and I could see nothing. Was he asleep?

I felt for the switch and turned it on. Light filled the room, and with it a cry of terror from my own breast.

On a chair in the middle of the room sat a gelatinous human figure that resembled Stosławski in its general form and facial features. But it was entirely transparent; the furniture behind it was plainly visible ...

Unable to believe my eyes, I touched it; it yielded under the pressure of my hand like a viscous liquid. Quickly I drew my hand back: the gooey, sticky substance slid off my fingers like gelatin and dribbled onto the floor.

All at once, the slimy form trembled in a strange, rippling manner and collapsed into pieces. Individual strands began to emerge from the transparent mass like ring nebulae which, having risen up, hovered for a brief time and then evaporated into space. After a few minutes there was nothing left – the chair was empty: Stosławski had vanished without a trace ...

My hair standing on end, I dashed out of the villa to the carriage and ordered it to depart at full speed. We drove in silence, illumined by the glow of the raging fire. Sarah asked no questions, and I did not feel like confiding in her.

When we reached the city, I put her up in a hotel and spent the night at my place.

The next day, I learned from the newspapers that the fire had fortunately been extinguished, and the villa spared. I hastened with the news to Sarah, who decided to return immediately. I drove her back, to live with her from then on, as was her fervent wish. I had agreed without hesitation. We did not talk about Stosławski, as if he had never existed. And so began the second phase of my acquaintance with this strange woman ...

I did not deviate so much as an inch from my former strategy. Although we lived together and had daily contact with one another, our relations did not take on a marital character. Although I had no direct evidence of the lethal influence that sexual intercourse with Sarah could have, my instincts warned me against excessive intimacy. So I played the role of a friend, ideal guardian, and advisor, carefully avoiding any kind of carnal union.

Sarah was clearly irritated by my stubbornness, which intensified her desire to break through it. She used a thousand means and half-measures which only an attractive woman could employ to overcome my resistance.

I must admit that at times I experienced moments of frenzied temptation – but whenever I called to mind the image of Stosławski, the horrible sight of his mortal remains lying there in that sumptuous bedroom, my hot-blooded passion turned straight to ice.

My curious self-restraint angered her at first: the first few months of our unnatural coexistence comprised a range of tumultuous scenes. When asked to explain myself, I blamed it on the platonic feelings I supposedly had for her.

'I value you too highly, Sarah, to dare avail myself of your body physically,' I often replied to her passionate outbursts. 'I have placed you on too high a pedestal to reach out and touch you. I don't want to defile my ideal.'

Then she would mock me, calling me a degenerate idealist or other even less flattering epithets. I endured these insults coolly, waiting to see how things would unfold.

And so a year passed. While at first Sarah had nurtured a hope that she would prevail, her confidence gradually eroded. That even her most ardent attacks had been ineffective no doubt baffled her – she began to look upon me with astonishment and – incredibly – a kind of fear. This fear revealed to me the reasons for her behavior. After a while, I became convinced that her desire to marry me was not driven solely by impulse, but had much deeper roots – most likely it was a matter of existence for her. It was fatal for her to yield to even a moment's physical attraction towards me – fatal for a woman who was used to winning, whom no man had thus far resisted. The moment she tightened her net around an individual

of the opposite sex, a special relationship was created for her that
carried an element of danger for both sides: it depended only on
the behavior of the man. If he yielded and consented to the sexual
act, Sarah had him in her grip forever. But if he remained aloof, the
situation could take a dangerous turn for this remarkable woman.
It seemed that in such a case she couldn't move casually into the
arms of another, couldn't freely untangle the reins to someone else
– until she had thrown the reluctant chosen one under her feet.
Hitherto her life had been a victory march, a ruthless triumph of
the subjugator. But the moment of reprisal had come, and I was its
instrument. Sarah Braga could not break free from me, could not
repel me, despite her futile efforts.

My resistance made me stronger every day; my unyielding
will intensified my power. After a year, the taunts and threats had
almost entirely disappeared, transforming into humble entreaties.
Sarah Braga – the proud, regal Sarah – had begun to beg and grovel
at my feet.

For it was her beauty, her appearance, her demonic youth that
was at stake; and maybe it was something more – maybe she was
begging for her life.

After a year of our living together, Sarah had begun to age visibly. One day I noticed insidious streaks of silver in her raven-black
hair and fresh wrinkles crisscrossing the corners of her mouth. Her
haughty figure was slowly losing its former elasticity, her breast
no longer flexing in supple waves. Sarah was wilting like a flower
in an autumn frost.

She was aware of this change – it was plain to see in any mirror
– and there were so many mirrors in the villa!

Then one day, to my inexpressible delight, I saw despair – hellish despair in her large, black, fiery eyes.

The fruits of my vengeance were ripening, catching up silently,
imperceptibly. My forces multiplied, surging powerfully as
though concentrating themselves within me. There was something inscrutable around me, assisting me; I had become a mag-
netic center, sucking in from the periphery the hidden energies
lying dormant in the house: I was not alone in the villa. These
mysterious symptoms began to evolve, currents previously sup-

pressed now asserted themselves more boldly, giving rise to new forces. But I could feel that they were sympathetic to me, that they had taken my side. And she recognized them – with horror, with the boundless terror of a hunted animal – and turned to me for refuge, for protection. How naïve! As if she didn't know that it was I who had released them.

From then on, she never wanted to sleep alone, fearfully waiting out the evening hours. The lights were left on all night long, keeping the villa as bright as day. She categorically refused to part from me for fear of being alone, superstitiously afraid of something terrible. And when she did fall asleep for a few hours, weary from her vigil, she would have terrifying dreams, as I could tell by her soft, stifled groaning.

Once, jumping out of bed in her nightdress with her hair undone, she flew to me in a mad fright and pressed her face against my breast, hands covering her face.

'What's wrong with you? Did you have a bad dream?' I asked, myself shaken with fear.

'I'm afraid,' she whispered, shaking like a leaf. 'I'm afraid. Just don't leave me alone here! I would die of fear in this house.'

If it were not for my firm obstinacy, she would have left the villa and moved elsewhere. But I enforced my will: she had to stay.

Finally, her fear, despair, and fits of impotent rage reached a tipping point. One night, gripped by a terrible nightmare, with her eyes spinning out of their orbits, she leapt out of bed in her nightshirt and stood over me, panting heavily. A breathless, wheezing whisper escaped from her mouth:

'Take me, you executioner! Take me or . . . die!' The blade of a Venetian dagger flashed coldly in her upraised hand.

I shot a glare at her: her paralyzed arm fell limply, the dagger slipping from her stiffened fingers.

'Ha, ha, ha!' I laughed, sitting down in the armchair where I had seen Stosławski's figure disappear for the last time.

'Ha, ha, ha! And, you see, I was prepared for that. You've asked me so many times why I despise your body, why I want nothing to do with you. I will respond by reading you something from the old holy books. Well, you can sit over there now – just don't try that again! It would be just as futile. Do you want to hear?'

With the resignation of a sacrificial victim awaiting the *coup de grâce*, she slumped down onto the carpet.

I opened a drawer and brought out a copy of the Old Testament, a book I had been studying avidly of late, immersing myself in its strange secrets, intoxicated by the poetry of its words and the profundity of its contents. I opened the Book of Kings and, in a calm voice imbued with the gravity of the moment, read aloud the following passage from the first chapter:

' "... Now King David was old, and advanced in years;

' "And they put covers on him, but he could not get warm.

' "Therefore his servants said to him: 'Let a young woman, a virgin, be sought for our lord the king, and let her stand before the king, and let her care for him; and let her lie in thy bosom, that the lord our king may be warm.

' "So they sought for a lovely young woman throughout all the territory of Israel, and found Abishag the Shunammite, and brought her to the King.

' "The young woman was very lovely, and she slept with the king and served him . . ." '

I paused, raising my eyes to Sarah. She avoided my gaze.

'Well, do you understand?'

She shrugged her shoulders nervously:

'What do I care? What does this passage have to do with us?'

'Don't lie to me, Sarah! You understand very well. This hoary old egotist – he is your forefather and master.'

'You're talking like a madman,' she answered, pursing her lips with emotion.

'You are lying, Sarah! But listen to the other excerpts from the Book of Tobit, chapters 3 and 6. These will explain the situation completely.'

'From the Book of Tobit?' she groaned, as if in her sleep.

'Yes, from the story of Tobit and Sarah; by a strange coincidence, you share a name with that devilish woman . . .

' "It came to pass the same day, that in Ecbatane, a city of Media, Sarah the daughter of Raguel was also reproached by her father's maids because she had been married to seven husbands, whom Asmodeus the evil spirit had killed, before they had lain with her . . ." '

Turning the page, I continued reading from chapter 6:

' "The angel said to the young man:

' " 'Brother, today we shall lodge with Raguel . . . he also hath one only daughter, named Sarah . . . I will speak for her, that she may be given thee for a wife.'

' "Then Tobit answered and said: 'I have heard . . . that this maid hath been given to seven men, who all died in the marriage chamber, and I hear also that the devil hath murdered them . . . and I am afraid, lest if I go in unto her, I die, as the others before . . .'

' "And the angel Raphael said unto him, 'Hearken unto me, and show me who these are to whom the devil can do violence. For those who marry in such a way that they cast God out of themselves . . . And take their fill of pleasure enough, like a horse and a mule, who have no sense . . . the devil has power over them . . .

' " 'But when thou takest her in marriage, entering into her bed-chamber, abstain from her for three days, and do nothing else but pray with her.' " '

I closed the Bible and looked at Sarah.

I will never forget her in that tragic moment. Despair and shame, rage, fear, and profound, incomprehensible pain crawled out of the abyss of that demonic soul to play one last time on her face with a jarring chord of dissonance!

Like a panther, she leapt towards me with predatorily curved fingers:

'You wicked scoundrel! You came here, destroyed me, trampled on me, and now you want to torment me further?'

I grabbed the tightly balled fist gearing up for a punch and disarmed it:

'Calm yourself, witch! Tonight is our last night together – tomorrow I will leave this house forever. But you will not spend the last few hours we have until dawn with me. I am sick of your company. Since you behave like a Fury, I'll leave you by yourself there in the living room. I want to rest here alone at last . . .' She resisted, and I dragged her almost violently amidst her persistent struggling into the brightly lit room. Then, having closed the door behind her, I returned to the bedroom and, my nerves rattled by the fight, leaned heavily against the window frame, staring into the black night . . .

Then the silence was broken by the loud, terrible, agonized scream of a woman. It was so shrill, so ear-piercing, that, despite everything, I rushed back into the living room.

It was dark inside. A moment before, the room had been awash in streams of light, but now it was submerged in the deep darkness of night: the electric lamps had suddenly gone out, the majestic chandeliers been extinguished. The screaming stopped abruptly, and there was a dull, stifling silence.

Overcome with indescribable fear, I retrieved a burning lamp from my bedroom and pointed it toward the raised platform . . . On the lowermost steps, Sarah was lying on her back with her arms crossed. Her eyes, glazed over with the stillness of death, looked out at me from a face contorted grotesquely in an expression of horror; she had died instantly under the influence of some inhuman terror.

Burning Ground

Rojecki reached for the large packet of letters on the tray; he opened one, scanned a few lines, then tossed it aside with disinterest.

'Old wives' tale,' he said, yawning, and moved on to the next.

'Not very interesting,' he mumbled after a second, setting this one aside also with evident discouragement.

He livened up a bit upon reading the third.

'Friend!', read the anonymous note, 'Down with superstitions! Let us leave them to old women and decadent weaklings. Do not waver once you have made up your mind. Enough of this hesitation!' It was signed, 'Well-Wisher'.

'Hmm,' he muttered thoughtfully, looking at the red signature of this 'Well-Wisher'. 'Hmm ...' Evidently people were very interested in this matter.

He got up from his chair, opened his desk drawer, and retrieved a large packet of earlier letters, wrapped in yellow paper. He removed a few and spread them on the desk in front of him.

'All of the same type,' he thought, comparing them with the one most recently received. 'Different handwriting, undoubtedly, yet the contents are almost identical throughout. And the anonymous signatures, all in red ink or colored pencil! Interesting! Interesting! What could it mean? A most comical and mysterious situation. The letters are written in standard black ink, but these pseudonymous signatures scream red ochre or minium. Some kind of red-lovers club, or what? Crazy chirographers!'

It was already starting to irritate him a bit. Ever since he had decided to build a villa in one of the remote districts of Kobryń, letters related to the matter had been flooding in from all over. The unsolicited advisors sending them could be grouped into two

opposing camps: one that Rojecki called 'the reds', who enthusiastically encouraged him to build the villa, and the other consisting
of individuals known to him personally or by reputation who
signed with their full name, and who earnestly advised against it,
trying at all costs to dissuade him from his 'mad' intention.

In general, the opponents of the enterprise inspired more trust
by showing their faces, as it were, rather than hiding behind false
names and mysterious initials. On the other hand, however, the
encouragement of the 'reds' had a certain sensational appeal for
him, awakening a vein of pugnacious defiance deeply hidden
beneath his public character as a hard-working archivist. Moreover, the rationale for the first group's warnings was based on
arguments that could not hold up to the scrutiny of a clear and
sober mind, which Andrzej Rojecki most certainly had.

Everything his acquaintances could offer in defense of their
position bore the hallmarks of old wives' tales, superstitions born
of an extraordinary series of coincidences. It should be noted that
their opinions on this matter evidently expressed the collective
opinion of the town as a whole. Rojecki recalled very well a conversation he had had a month after his arrival in Kobryń with a
craftsman not far from 'that place'.

It was around eight o'clock in the evening when Rojecki,
weary from a full day's work, was walking slowly along a narrow,
upward-sloping street. He was scouting out a place to build a villa,
his professional interests requiring him to settle for an indefinite
period in this filthy and unappealing city. Feeling alienated in
hotels, and in his current lodgings on Długa Street, he had decided
to build a home for himself and his family somewhere far from the
squalid city center. He just could not determine exactly where.

He spent a week wandering around the outskirts of the city, but
could not find any suitable place. Finally he ventured westward
down Czarna Street, which eventually led to a suburban meadow.

He had passed the last single-story homes, and then the glass-
works, and was turning right into the meadow when his attention
was drawn to a circular cluster of fir trees on a small elevation near
the river.

The place instantly appealed to him. The location was beau-

tiful, far from the noises and stench of the city – against a background of green meadows and hay fields, and the bluish wall of
forest in the distance.

Rojecki crossed the footbridge erected over the river, which
partially encircled the hill of fir trees, and began walking up the
hill. A set of stone steps made for a rather convenient passage to the
top. The ring of firs and spruces was so dense that Rojecki initially
couldn't see anything through it. Only when he walked around to
the northern side of the hill did he find an opening through which
he could pass. Here, a sad sight stretched out before him. The area
enclosed by the trees was a pile of burnt ruins.

Here and there, charred beams jutted out of the stone founda-
tions; on both sides of the remaining walls, which seemed ready to
collapse at the slightest gust of wind, sections of curled wallpaper
stuck out like flayed skin; there was no trace of any roof, save for
an iron bar which had probably supported the vaulted ceiling, and
which now traced a black diagonal line over the ruins of the interior.

There were details to suggest that the home had been furnished
with particular luxuriousness, and that it could lay claim to a certain elegance and good taste. There remained untouched on the
grounds a bower of plaited wild grapevines, two Greek statuettes
in the flowerbeds, and a red pyrite cistern. Suspended between two
pines, a rope swing rocked gently in the evening wind.

Oddly, the fire did not appear to have touched any of the spruce
trees which surrounded the house at some distance.

'A wonderful spot,' Rojecki thought as he approached what
remained of a stone terrace.

Just then, he heard the sound of iron being struck from behind
one of the remaining walls.

'Someone's here,' he whispered, moving toward the noise. Just
as he was about to cross the blackened frame of the former entryway, a rather pitiable-looking man leaned out from behind a pile
of beams and tipped his cap in greeting.

'Good evening, sir!'

'Good evening! Any chance you'd happen to know who the
owner of this unfortunate place was?'

'Indeed, I do. The owner of the house when it burned down

five years ago was a Mr. Dołżycki, an engineer, who then moved to America. Five years these ruins have been sitting here, untouched since the day after the fire. I noticed a couple of iron support anchors from the exterior corners here in the rubble, and I came here today to pick them up; they're of no use to anyone, and I just happen to be a carpenter and builder by profession.'

'Oh, yes, I understand. I just find it a bit strange that no one's rebuilt on this spot yet. Seems a waste of space – such a beautiful location, a picturesque little corner. Did this Dołżycki leave any instructions regarding the place prior to his departure?'

'As far as I know,' said the craftsman, 'he handed it over to the municipality, free of charge.'

'Free? A place as fine as this, and after such a loss?'

The carpenter smiled enigmatically.

'It's not like he would have found a buyer. As I said, it's been five years, and no one's been keen to snatch it up. No surprise there; why set yourself up for a sure loss? Everyone knows that Dołżycki wasn't the first to have gotten burned on the deal. Well, no use going on about it – it's a burning ground, and that's that.'

'A burning ground? I don't understand. I guess you mean a burnt-up place?'

'No, my friend. A burning ground; I know what I'm talking about. It's different from a burnt-up place. People around here call this place a burning ground because not a single house erected here has lasted without burning down. As far back as local memory goes, every building, no matter how shoddy, has gone up in flames here on this hill. Some say that none has lasted more than four months. Ptui!' he added, spitting on the ground, 'an unclean place, is what it is!'

The archivist smiled incredulously:

'It's certainly an interesting coincidence. It almost seems as though fire really has it in for this place.'

The carpenter was offended.

'Not "as though", sir, and it doesn't just "seem" so – it really does. Not the whole hill, since you can see it hasn't touched these firs, but only the very center of it, in other words, exactly where the houses have been built.'

'Well, well,' continued Rojecki with interest, 'what about yourself, how many fires do you recall happening here?'

The craftsman thought for a moment.

'Ten,' he said finally. 'I can recall ten times that a fire has broken out here. And I'm thirty years old.'

'Wow!' Rojecki was genuinely surprised. 'That's an average of one every three years.'

'Somehow that's how it's turned out. Apparently they burned more frequently in the past, before people figured out what was going on. The oldest residents of Kobryń remember those times well, you could learn a lot talking to them – they've got some strange stories about this accursed hill. That's why no one from this area has been eager to build anything up here. In my time, the owners of the houses have been foreigners to the region who knew nothing about all this, or like Dołżycki, who didn't want to know.'

'Were the causes of the fires always discovered?'

'Well, yes and no. Most often it's been soot catching fire in the chimney, but there have also been other "causes": once, someone carelessly tossed a match, which anywhere else would have burned quietly down to the end without causing a fire; another time, by some "accident", a cigarette butt fell into a bundle of straw beneath a bed; and yet another time, a burning lamp overturned onto a pillow. This last blaze apparently broke out due to the carelessness of Mrs. Dołżycki herself, who was cleaning her gloves with petrol while sitting too close to a burning candle. Always some moment of foolishness, a mere trifling mistake that anywhere else would have had no effect; but here, my friend – a fire so fierce that people barely escape with their lives, and which makes going inside to save them impossible. Firemen say that each time it's been as though something hindered their attempts to put it out, and that it burned like the devil; they hate having to come here, because very few of them leave unscathed, without burns or some other serious injury . . .'

'Have you ever witnessed one of these fires yourself?' interrupted Rojecki.

'I have. Several, in fact; I live close by here. I even have a fine little souvenir from the last one.'

He rolled up his shirt sleeve, displaying a large, deep scar on his arm.

'This is my punishment for helping in the rescue attempts. Some devilish rafter fell and almost crushed my hand. It's not good, sir, to attempt to save anyone while the fire's burning. It takes its revenge on folks afterward. Staszek Luśnia, a cartwright from across the river, and Wałek Wron, a tailor's apprentice, both volunteered as firemen during two of the previous blazes, and had fires at their homes a few days later which they just barely managed to extinguish. So now, no one from town besides the professional firemen will come out to help here, for fear that something terrible might happen to them. Best not to antagonize evil. Anyway, I'm pretty sure everyone within a hundred miles knows about this place, and you won't find anyone willing to settle here.'

'And yet . . .' said Rojecki thoughtfully, 'and yet, who knows? Perhaps some willing person might yet be found. People can be stubborn.'

The craftsman looked astonished.

'Maybe a madman, or a half-wit. Throwing away all that money just to put his life in danger.'

'Hm.' The archivist smiled meaningfully. 'Not necessarily, my good man, not necessarily. One just has to be careful, that's all.'

With that, Rojecki took his leave of the man and returned to the city. A few days later he signed a contract at the town hall, thereby taking ownership, at a fantastically low price, of the 'burning ground'. While filling out the paperwork, the archivist noticed the bemused faces and knowing smiles of the officials. One of them, a kindly fellow with a full head of gray hair, pulled him aside and quietly advised against the purchase:

'It's an unlucky place,' he explained, stammering. 'A piece of land under a bad star. Haven't you heard anything about it?'

'I may have,' Rojecki responded, unmoved, 'but I don't believe in such nonsense. In any case, thank you, sir, for your kind intentions.'

He shook hands with the man and left the office.

On the following day, the first two letters arrived: one from a judge with whom he was acquainted, advising against building the house, and the other from one of the 'reds', full of enthusiasm for the enterprise. From there, the letters proceeded to pour in as from a horn of plenty. It seemed that the whole town was talking of nothing else but the fact that Andrzej Rojecki, the archivist who had arrived only a month before, was going to build a house on the 'burning ground.'

And he did build it. Tired of the intrusive correspondence of these advisors, he resolved to quickly and decisively 'cut the head off the hydra' and free himself from the prying of his neighbors. The desire to show this 'little world' how one can cast off superstitions and grind old wives' tales into dust also played a role.

A few days after signing the deed he informed his wife, who had stayed behind in Warsaw with their ten-year-old son Józef, about the proceedings. Mrs. Rojecki wrote back to say that of course she approved of his plan, and that she would depart for Kobryń as soon as the house was finished. Like her husband, she put no stock in the rumors surrounding the place, branding them several times in her letter as 'simple-minded nonsense' and 'small-town superstitions'.

Satisfied with her response, Rojecki summoned a renowned Warsaw architect to Kobryń the following week, under whose personal supervision the construction began. It proceeded swiftly, with the archivist sparing no expense, and within two months a beautiful Art Nouveau-style villa stood atop the hill of firs.

Rojecki christened the building with the provocative name of 'Blaze Manor'. Construction was completed at the tail end of spring, and by the beginning of July, the Rojecki family had moved in.

Maria Rojecki was delighted with her little provincial nest, and immediately made herself at home there. Józef, a blue-eyed little scamp, quickly embarked on an adventurous expedition deep into the virginal Brazilian forest, as he liked to call the fir grove surrounding the villa, and was soon thrilled to discover that red squirrels, and perhaps even deer, lived within it.

The hill, quiet for so many years, now resonated with laughter and the buzz of cheerful voices. Even Nero, the large watchdog with a white patch on his ear, seemed more than pleased with his new doghouse beside the trees, judging by his playful barking and vigorous tail-wagging.

The family decided not to make use of the house's kitchen; Marianna, formerly the cook, now took on the position of housemaid. They ate lunch and dinner at one of the first-rate restaurants in town, or had meals delivered to them. This arrangement, while somewhat inconvenient, Mr. Rojecki considered necessary for safety's sake; with no flames being lit in the kitchen, one of the most likely causes of a conflagration was thus eliminated.

For, despite his level-headed views on this 'poppycock', Rojecki promised himself that he would be careful. Having cast aside with contempt all explanations hinging on the 'unnaturalness' of the place, he had 'found' a natural cause against which his common sense did not rebel; in his view, the abnormal frequency of the blazes could be attributed simply to the particular atmospheric conditions of the place. It seemed likely that the space, enclosed as it was by so many firs and spruces, was exceptionally saturated with oxygen. People did not realize this at first and were careless, and then ... and then ... Here there was a momentary, but rather unpleasant, break in Rojecki's line of reasoning, which he proceeded to fill in more or less as follows: And then, these silly stories about an 'unlucky place', along with this ridiculous, superstitious fear, had a kind of autosuggestive effect which compelled people to act negligently, stimulated them to commit certain unconscious actions: an involuntary movement of the hands, a disastrous moment of clumsiness, and then ... a fire breaks out.

For this reason, Rojecki resolved to be cautious, even excessively so. He was dead set on breaking the chain of superstition encircling his current place of residence and disrupting the cycle of fires once and for all by dousing them with fresh cold water.

Oil lamps, candles, alcohol burners, and other similar lighting implements were strictly forbidden at Blaze Manor. Instead, electricity was fed to the building from the local trolley station in a single current that branched throughout the house, providing light and warmth throughout. Breakfast and late-afternoon snacks were heated on an electric stove with a whole network of powerful resistors.

Rojecki only used a gas lighter to light cigarettes and cigars, doing so with the utmost precaution: he typically stood at the center of the room, at a safe distance from the furnishings. During the first few weeks, it was rather difficult for Rojecki to adjust to all of these arrangements and this new household routine, but in time he got used to it. And life flowed on in Blaze Manor on the calm, pleasant waves of everyday routine.

Rojecki worked in the municipal archives from eight o'clock until afternoon, then returned home, where he spent the rest of the day 'in the bosom of his family'. The proximity of the forest, only two kilometers from the river, allowed for frequent late-afternoon excursions, from which the Rojeckis would return home refreshed and in good spirits. On overcast days, they would stroll the white-gravel paths that wound through the fir grove. Somewhere on the slope, Józef discovered a couple of granite blocks through which a small stream trickled; the clever boy rearranged the stones so that they formed a kind of basin, creating a small well – the destination of frequent jaunts, and a source of refreshment on sweltering summer days . . .

Meanwhile, the family and their 'Blaze Manor' remained the most popular topic of conversation among the townsfolk. There was no church fair or evening gathering at which they weren't gossiped about. The Rojeckis themselves seldom took part in these events, if only because Kobryń society kept its distance from Blaze Manor. People were afraid to spend even two hours in the dangerous villa. To his great pleasure, Rojecki noticed the curious faces of his colleagues who greeted him every morning at work; there was obvious astonishment in the eyes and expressions of these good-hearted folk:

'How is everything, my good sir? No fire yet?'

Every couple of days some casual acquaintance, encountering him in the street, would look him compassionately in the eye and, with a warm clasp of the hand and a tone of gentle concern, inquire:

'How have you been, my dear Andrzej? Nothing strange has happened to you yet?'

The archivist would laugh heartily as he recounted these encounters to his wife. But there were also a few brave souls who did visit Blaze Manor from time to time; these were chiefly old bachelors with 'nothing to lose'. But even they spent their time there on tenterhooks, as it were, casting wild glances around like a cornered animal. Such guests always put Rojecki in a fine humor. Finally Rojecki suggested to one of them that he avoid coming to Blaze Manor unless escorted by the volunteer fire department. Then the guest took offense and didn't come again . . .

And so the sweltering days of July and August passed without incident, then September, with its bountiful harvest, and the cobwebbed days of October were nearing their end. Nothing 'happened' at Blaze Manor. It was then that a clear shift in public opinion occurred. People began to look upon the inhabitants of the lonely villa with manifest admiration and respect. For as long as Kobryń had been Kobryń, no house constructed on the burning ground had ever lasted more than four months, and here the fourth month was coming to an end, and all was quiet . . . October passed, and a melancholy November began. Rojecki rubbed his hands with satisfaction, accepting with an indulgent smile the congratulations of his friends on having 'fortunately survived the critical period.' Guests began to visit more often, and to stay longer; gradually their unease and nervous movements disappeared. It was nice and cheerful in Blaze Manor because the hosts turned out to be very hospitable people. The mood changed from pleasant and agreeable to almost exaggeratedly boisterous, jocular, and champagne-fueled. Rojecki mercilessly mocked their superstitions and smiled triumphantly, while Mrs. Rojecki teased the judge's wife on the subject of 'unlucky' days and places. Józef ran wild through the forest and the neighborhood; even Marianna, now the 'housemaid', usually a stolid and serious woman, now cracked jokes in the kitchen and laughed at just about anything.

Gradually, imperceptibly, new preferences and habits began to emerge in the household.

'*C'est drôle!*' the beautiful Mrs. Sulimirska remarked one day upon returning from a visit to Blaze Manor. 'Mrs. Rojecki has been wearing a fiery red peignoir for some time now; it's the fifth time this week she's entertained us in this color!'

It was an astute observation. The Rojeckis had indeed taken a particular liking to red and red-orange hues; Maria had been wearing dresses in these colors exclusively for the past month, with only small variations in shade and nuance. Her husband noted with pleasure that this suited her and, deciding to take on a similar style himself, began to wear flashy, fiery ties.

'And his color is red,' one of his friends said the following day, humming an air from 'La Marseillaise'.

'Nothing wrong with that,' he answered calmly. 'I like this color. It fits me, just as it fits my wife. That's all there is to it.'

And a few days later, he exchanged his tie for another one in a brick-red hue.

Even Józef seemed to adopt his parents' taste in colors, beginning to request new clothes in those shades. And so, on the occasion of his birthday shortly afterward, they bought him a red suit.

As if to follow through with this style to its fullest extent, toward the end of November, Andrzej Rojecki ordered all the rooms to be covered in red wallpaper with a pattern of deep-yellow irises.

'What a pleasant, warm shade this is now,' said his wife, after this interior metamorphosis.

'Isn't that right, my darling?' he said, kissing her beautiful, velvety eyes. 'Warmth seems to flow from the walls – a blissful, soul-warming heat.'

But in town, these changes were considered eccentric, and the county doctor Lutowski even described them as a kind of so-called erythromania. By some unknown means, Rojecki became aware of this description, giving him occasion for renewed mockery:

'These simple folk,' he confided to his wife, 'accuse us of some kind of madness for the color red, pathetically ignorant of the fact that they themselves have fallen victim to fire-mania of a much more serious sort.'

'That's true,' Maria agreed, staring at the iron coils of the electric radiator beside the wall. 'In general, I have the impression that all of these precautions we've been following here are really entirely superfluous, even downright ridiculous. For example now, looking at these dead radiator tubes as dark waves of heat run through them, I find myself longing for our good old stoves. How sweet it was to chat beside a crackling fire, with its red reflections playing on the walls...'

'How right you are, Maria. I've been thinking the same thing. But it is not too late. Tomorrow, I'll have some stoves installed; we'll have our fire, along with the scent of resinous pitch and rocketing sparks.'

'Hooray!' shouted Józef, beaming with joy. 'We'll have stoves! We'll have fire! Fantastic fire – gold, red, yellow! Oh how wonderful, how beautiful, daddy!'

By early December, the villa was being heated in the traditional manner by means of tile stoves, and in the salon a jolly fire blazed in the large, old Polish fireplace.

This fundamental breach of the prior tactics was soon followed by others. Rojecki, emboldened by the absence of any dire consequence, became ever more brazen. In December, they stopped taking their meals in town, and restored the *ancien régime* of home cooking; Marianna very happily resumed her gastronomic duties.

'And rightly so, my good lord and lady,' she opined as she brought her home-cooked supper into the dining room for the first time. 'A crying shame it is, lunching and dining out in taverns. With a kitchen as good as gold at home, and dishes shining on the walls like diamonds – here we've been, carting this dreck home from restaurants as though we've no one to cook for us. A real crime!'

This rebellious reaction brought about swift developments. In the evenings, they began using 'good old' oil lamps, in addition to the electric lighting; Mrs. Rojecki soon decidedly preferred them when reading music and sewing, claiming that the electric ones were bad for her eyesight. Candles also reappeared in the home after a long absence. In a word, old-fashioned lighting and heating won a decisive victory in Blaze Manor over more modern technologies.

On long winter evenings the family would gather around the fireplace, which became the center of their domestic life. The hearth, glowing red with the heat of logs and kindling, exerted an irresistible influence on them, drawing them in with the power of this mysterious element. They sat for hours in silence staring into the bloody abyss, engrossed in the sounds of crackling wood and bursts of sparks. The spell of the flames had a particularly strong effect on Andrzej and Józef; they outdid one another in stoking the fire, often adding fresh fuel when none was needed.

'Dad,' the boy confessed one evening, 'one of these days, I'd like to have a big, huge bonfire, like the one the shepherds light in the fields in autumn.' He turned to his mother, whose eyes were fixed on the flames as she played some wild rhapsody. 'Mom – isn't it true that fire is beautiful – so very beautiful?'

'It is true, son,' she responded, listening to the fiery melody. Then, as though interpreting her child's enchantment with the dangerous element, she began to play an aria from Verdi's *Il trovatore*.

'*Con fuoco!*' Rojecki encouraged, accompanying her with his fine baritone. '*Con fuoco! Più di fuoco.*'

'*Stride la vampa . . .*'

Józef's fanatical fire-worship took on a childish form appropriate to his age. On several occasions his parents noticed him lighting a candle in broad daylight, then sitting for hours playing with the flame. Another time, Andrzej entered his bedroom to find a pile of papers and newsprint aflame on a table, while Józef looked on in delight.

A few days later, while tidying the boy's room, Marianna was horrified to find some partially charred object under the bed, wrapped in a small patterned rug. Investigations by Mrs. Rojecki found that this mysterious burnt thing was one of Andrzej's old chessboards, which Józef had secretly sacrificed to the flames.

The boy trembled in fear of his father's wrath and hid himself away in some little nook – but to everyone's surprise, Rojecki received the news of this crime with unusual forbearance, offering not even the slightest reproach.

The archivist was much like his son in his affection for fire; he 'understood' Józef's passion and even – strangely enough – envied him for the simple ways he was able to satisfy it. Andrzej was soon to surpass him.

Some time in the middle of January, he came up with the idea of 'fire games'. One day while his wife was giving Józef piano lessons in the parlor, Rojecki decided to arrange a little 'surprise'. Quietly, without drawing attention to himself, he sneaked a bottle

of spirits into the bedroom and poured all of its contents onto one
of the pillows; then he set fire to it . . .

An intense fire broke out, consuming the bedcovers in the blink
of an eye; delighted with the effect, Andrzej called the other 'players' into the room. Maria gave a cry of admiration and, clutching
her son's hand, began staring fixedly at the tongues of fire lashing
the drapes.

The master of the house was the first to wake from his trance,
having been standing with arms crossed watching the progress of
the flames. With a terrible laugh, he rushed to extinguish them,
removing the mattress along with a heavy Turkish blanket from
the adjacent bed and violently flinging them over the burning heap.
The attempt was successful; the snaking flames of bright azure
were stifled instantly, slithering somewhere beneath the bedclothes
and expiring. But Rojecki was not deceived by appearances. With
the zeal of a fireman he launched a second attack, suffocating the
strands of pale blue fire that crept out treacherously from below.
Before the chastened elemental force could recover, he mounted a
third and final assault, this time with water from buckets that Marianna had brought just in the nick of time. The fire was quenched.
Andrzej stood for some time with his fists clenched anxiously, not
saying a word, watching the burnt-up bedclothes and half-charred
bed. Suddenly he let out a strange, uneasy laugh:

'Ha, ha! We've had a "blaze" in "Blaze Manor"! Haven't we,
Maria? And we smothered it with our own hands, without help
from anybody – our own bare hands. We strangled that red hydra,'
he added after a moment, in a low voice. 'Ha, ha, ha! Well, Józef?
Wasn't that great?'

And then the three of them sat down for supper as though
nothing had happened. Late in the evening, as they lay down to
sleep in the heavily damaged bedroom, Maria whispered in her
husband's ear:

'And yet, my love, fire is such a beautiful element . . .'

From then on, 'surprises' began to happen more and more often
in Blaze Manor. With the zeal of a mischievous child, Rojecki
would play these 'fire pranks' on his family without any regard for
the enormous losses they suffered as a result. He was enormously

entertained by the act of unleashing this element, which he knew
how to rein in at the critical moment, and was especially delighted
every time he successfully vanquished this perfidious enemy.

Fire had destroyed half of the bedroom, reduced a number of
expensive objects to coal, and consumed a large portion of the
family's clothing. The Rojeckis regarded all of this with indifference, desiring only fiery emotions, thirsting for 'red sensations'.

But the archivist assiduously concealed his 'games' from the
outside world; Marianna, under threat of immediate expulsion
from the household, was forbidden from talking to anyone in
town about what had happened in the villa. Oddly Rojecki, who
was so free in his pursuits before his wife and child, seemed to be
ashamed of his 'predilections' before the outside world.

The damage in the house resulting from these intentional fires
was repaired covertly and with great care. Whenever unexpected
visitors showed up, singed furnishings were quickly removed and
any suggestive traces diligently washed away, or the clever Marianna would immediately lead the guests to a room away from any
affected areas.

But this constant concealment and the necessity for caution in
dealings with his neighbors took the wind out of Rojecki's sails.
Eventually he tired of it and decided to play a prank on his guests
that would also serve as an act of revenge.

One Sunday, while a large group was being entertained in the
drawing room at Blaze Manor, a candle caused the curtain hanging over the living-room doorway to catch fire. Someone cried
'Fire!' and a terrible panic ensued. A couple of ladies fainted, others
jumped from the windows in their formal wear, insufficiently
dressed for the 20-degree frost outside. Within a few seconds
Rojecki had put the fire out and, with a sardonic smile, began inviting the frightened guests back inside. But the people were in no
mood for further entertainment and hurriedly departed for their
homes, ushered off by the ironic gaze of the master of the house.

'You've seen for yourselves, ladies and gentlemen,' said the
implacable Rojecki as he bade them farewell. 'Well? Is fire really so
terrible here at the "burning ground"?'

'Yes, yes, you're right, my dear Andrzej; the energy you showed in vanquishing that accursed element was admirable,' one or another of them replied. 'But it is better, my dear sir, not to trifle with fire; you can never be too careful.'

And then they furtively made their way out of the villa . . .

February passed, and gusty March began. Rojecki was still playing with fire. But gradually, the motives behind his amusements had changed. While at first it was all about the pleasure of smothering and defeating the unbridled element, his satisfaction at the taste of victory gave way to an insurmountable lust for fire for its own sake. Because of this, he put off quenching them for longer and longer, giving the flames a chance to unfold more freely. He first had to revel in the sight of the raging fire before coming to the rescue. This meant that some blazes were left burning up to the critical moment, and the game really became something of a gamble. Despite this, and regardless of the danger posed to his family, Andrzej was never satisfied – it always felt as though he had begun to extinguish the blaze too early, and that it was possible to dial up the tension a notch. For some reason he felt that all of these 'rehearsals' were merely a prelude to something greater, just a pale foreshadowing of 'fun in grand style'.

And he was not wrong. The longed-for moment would soon come. It happened on March 19th, St. Joseph's Day.

That night, the Rojeckis returned home from a boisterous party at the Warecki home. Maria, exhausted by countless waltzes, quickly fell into a deep slumber. Rojecki couldn't sleep. He lit a cigarette and, lying on his back, gave himself up to the indistinct visions unfolding behind his closed eyelids.

Slowly, the images began to come together and coalesce, until they merged into the clear, unmistakable contours of a building in flames.

Rojecki recognized the building. It was the Doge's Palace in Venice, which he had seen years before during his wanderings abroad. Now he saw it engulfed in violet flames against the black background of a stifling midsummer's night.

Why this particular building? He didn't know. But he could distinctly feel the heat of the blaze, smell the stench of burning, as though he were very close to it, only a few steps away . . .

He raised himself up out of bed and automatically lit a candle. Taking it in his hand, he opened a trunk and began searching inside. Finally he removed a string-tied bundle which had been prepared some time ago. He untied the string. Coils of oakum spilled out . . .

He gathered a clump of it, bunched it up under the wardrobe, then set it aflame. Without looking back, he went into the drawing room, tossed a pile of the coarse fiber underneath an armchair and, having touched the candle flame to it, crept into the dining room as though in a dream state. He quickly managed to set the kitchen table alight; then, choking on the smoke, he spread the tinder around the living room. As he passed through to the bathroom, a powerful blast of flames from the alcove blocked his way. He let out a short, nervous laugh and disappeared down the hallway, a clump of flaming flax tow in his hand . . .

The next morning alarm bells rang out in Kobryń.

'It's burning, it's burning!' frightened voices cried. Fearful faces appeared in windows, people rushed out into the street. The bells went on tolling their protracted, funereal groans.

'Jesus, Mary!' a woman yelled. 'A fire at the burning ground! Rojecki's in flames!'

'He won't get out alive!'

'His time has finally come!'

People said their farewells superstitiously, staring in amazement at the massive red column rising up above the fir trees on the hill at the edge of town . . .

But no one rushed to help; fear had pinned their feet to the ground, arrested their movements, frozen their will . . .

From far off, the firemen's trumpet call sounded. Soon, a pair of fire engines and carts carrying rescue personnel were speeding to the site. They arrived within a quarter of an hour . . . too late! The villa was one big ocean of flames. Tongues of fire flicked from the windows, flared out of the doors through clouds of smoke, shot up in bloody barbs over the chimneys. And nearby, Andrzej Rojecki was running around like a maniac in his underwear holding an ax, cutting down the firs and spruces with a kind of demonic joy, foaming at the mouth as he dragged them and fed them to the fire . . .

Some of the braver firemen managed to enter the house, only to return some time later carrying three charred bodies: two women and a child. Rojecki resisted violently until he could be subdued and bound with ropes, then was carted off to a mental institution.

Parable of the Tunnel Mole

For as long as anyone can remember, the Florek family has served as guardians of the railway tunnel running under Turbacz in the Gorce Mountains. This function, not at all an appealing one, somehow became hereditary in their family, passing from father to son. Supposedly it's now the fourth generation in a row whose members guard the depths beneath the mountain. They were born here, spent their lives here in hard watchman's service, then died here. It was only death, that great leveler of people, professions, and things, that tore them out of the stony guts of the mountain and gave them up to the ground and the refuge of the cemetery, bathed in sunlight here and there despite the shade cast by the mountain peaks. Death – the common steward of human fates and human fortunes . . .

The most recent watchman of the Florek clan was Antoni, son of Jan, who had died suddenly fifteen years earlier while setting a switch. The current guard was at that time a youth of about twenty, already well versed in the arcana of his trade, having been initiated by his father into his predestined role as successor. Therefore, immediately after the death of his aged parent and master, he took over his duties as a tunnel guard. It was as natural as the succession of day after night, spring after winter. There was no objection on the part of the railway authorities, who did not require of their new watchman any special 'test' or 'internship'. What would be the point, anyway? He had been practicing the trade since the age of sixteen, assisting his father with efficiency and skill, as befits the son of an old railwayman. So why would anyone bother him by imposing conditions and piling on pointless requirements for purely theoretical purposes?

Especially since no one else was eager to perform this thankless service, for to be a watchman in the tunnel under Turbacz meant to renounce life and sunshine. Working on the narrow, six-kilometer line, forged by human ingenuity out of the rocky subsoil, required a level of sacrificial self-denial pushed to the utmost limit.

Years ago, before the Florek family took over the position, there had been a change of guard. Every six days a watchman from the nearest stop at Krzywy Wirch would come and 'relieve' his colleague from the tunnel for twenty-four hours; thus, every six days the prisoner of Turbacz was freed to look upon the sun and light of day. Every six days!

This is how things were before the Florek family descended into the depths of the tunnels. As soon as Andrzej, progenitor of this lineage of watchmen, first took on the position, this hundred-year custom abruptly ceased. From then on, only members of the Florek family performed these underground duties, entrusting the role of temporary substitute only to their children and grandchildren. In the surrounding villages and mountainous abodes, it was widely claimed that they had arranged with the authorities to reserve the changing of the guard among themselves, limiting the role to forces drawn from the bosom of their own family.

The powers that be complied with their wishes, readily approving of this self-sufficient operation. The state treasury could only benefit from it, and the function be performed more efficiently. Service in the tunnels, carried out year after year by members of the same family, became an organic, peculiar, highly individualized activity. Their practical nature had the effect of removing the mechanized and soulless routine of the role, infusing it with the vigor of class interest in the 'cause', ensuring it was performed ardently, even enthusiastically. So it was that over time, the subterranean railway under Turbacz came to be known as the 'Florek tunnel' . . .

Unfortunately, at present the family was on the brink of extinction. The current watchman, Antoni, already thirty-five years old, was its final, infertile offspring. He had no wife, and no desire for one; and so the Florek family line was irrevocably approaching its end . . .

Antoni Florek was a strange man. He was below average in

height, with an unusually pale complexion and hair as light as flax, nearly white. His eyes were peculiar: small, black, and beady, with a red rim around the irises, they squinted tensely when exposed to light, narrowing to slits like those of a cat. This last of the Florek line could not stand sunlight.

Born in the semi-darkness of a tunnel illuminated only by the artificial light of electric lamps, he hated the light of day. This child of the underworld had been saddled with the curse of atavism, the centuries-old form of existence passed down from his ancestors. Antoni Florek had never once looked upon the disc of the sun. His only attempt to peer out from the gloomy depths of the tunnels years ago had almost cost him his sight. Compelled by curiosity, he had wandered close to the mouth of the tunnel and was so powerfully dazzled that he ended up completely blind for several hours. Having with difficulty groped his way back into the subterranean depths, he spent the rest of that dreadful afternoon in the darkest corners of the tunnels, a blindfold covering his stricken eyes. For the next several days he felt intense pain in his brow ridges and saw everything as through a thick iron grate. From then on, whenever his duties required him to venture near any of the exits, he always wore a pair of dark-green glasses. He avoided them as much as possible, preferring to hide in the depths of his native territory. That occasion had developed in him a visceral aversion toward the sun and the light of day, so that nothing in the world could persuade him to depart from his underground burrows even for a moment.

He felt comfortable there, safe and at home. The painful experience had forever extinguished whatever minimal interest he might have had in what lay outside the bounds of the tunnel.

The only connections he had with the outside world were the trains that passed six times a day through the tunnels, and a sickly, halfwitted boy of fifteen by the name of Jędruch who came every other day to bring him only the most necessary of provisions. Otherwise, Antoni Florek entertained no visitors in his gloomy solitude, being a sullen individual who shunned human companionship. Since the death of his father he had hardly exchanged a word with anyone, communicating only by signs with the idiot-boy Jędruch, who was a deaf-mute. It was even rumored that

Antoni had forgotten human speech as a consequence of his long silence, and that it would be very difficult to communicate with him today. A few years earlier, when a broken axle on one of the carriages forced an express train to stop in the tunnel for a time and its conductor tried to engage the stubbornly silent railwayman in conversation, Florek replied only reluctantly and with great difficulty, like a man struggling to find words to express his thoughts . . .

It was only in times of solitude and silence, during hours undisturbed by the passage of trains, that the watchman felt wholly within his element. His hunched back would straighten, his timidly bowed head raise up, and his small, constricted pupils light up with a flash of renewed vigor.

For Antoni Florek loved his stony underground realm with the passion of the solitary and the sick. He loved the low, barrel-shaped vault, the weight of this granite colossus hanging over him, pressing down upon him; he loved the sloping walls, roughly hewn through the body of living rock; he loved the immense, profound silence, and the shadow-drenched, eternally somber scenery . . .

There lay concealed in them something inscrutable, a dense and obstinate force, a kind of power born of stillness, and menacing by its inertia.

Florek felt, with the instinct of a child of the underworld, that half-light was the most appropriate lighting for a place governed by such a mysterious power, if not absolute darkness. Therefore, taking advantage of the long intervals between trains, he would lower the light in the tunnels by half, and even sometimes to a third of their expected brightness. According to regulations, the six-kilometer tunnel under Turbacz had to be fully illuminated day and night by electric lamps spaced at regular intervals of sixty meters. To the watchman, however, this lighting felt much too intense, and therefore unnecessary. As soon as a train completed its passage through the second part of the tunnel, which is to say, from his guard post to the exit, he would promptly 'roll back' the 'excess' lighting. This had the effect of creating a gloomy atmosphere appropriate to the mood he was trying to induce. There were regions of total blackness, small alleyways of darkness so profound as to completely inhibit sight, and then again zones of dubious illumination, at the crossroads of light and darkness, enigmatic and uncertain spaces, full of possibility. Only in the depths, at the very heart of the tunnel, did there burn, like an eternal and unchanging flame, a lamp illuminating the watchman's post – a tiny building set back in a rocky alcove with signaling and telegraphic equipment, along with a trio of switches. This was the place Florek liked the least, an 'official' area which, despite outward appearances, was the only 'black' spot in the whole tunnel. He was only a guest there.

He would appear at his post a few minutes before a train was due to arrive and adjust the lighting to meet the 'official' standards; then, assuming the stereotypical bearing of an official on duty, take up his position at the signal box. After fifteen minutes of tiresome waiting, when the rumblings of the iron monster had faded off into the distance, the residual echoes had dampened, and the rocky crags and recesses returned to their slumber, he would eagerly toss aside the signal board, dim the lights, and retreat into the darkest regions of the tunnel.

He didn't even spend the nights in his guardhouse, preferring to rest his head for a few hours in one of the dark, moist, and cool granite recesses than in the tiny room which, though warm and cozy, pained him with its excessive lighting.

As the years passed, whatever had any connection with the outside world, by reminding him of it and therefore imposing it upon him, became loathsome and repulsive. Florek hated the guardhouse, hated the railway apparatuses surrounding it, hated the ribbon of dual rail lines, because these were artifacts of 'those from outside', things that originated from 'the surface'. Those times when a train passed through the tunnel were moments of the greatest agony for him. He could not stand those loud, steam-panting monsters and the metallic clatter of their wheels over the rails. They spoiled the atmosphere, disturbing the silence that had slumbered down there for centuries and which was so dear to him. So he would close his eyes the moment they passed his guardpost and let them glide by, like the illusory yet malevolent images one sees in dreams . . .

For what did he care about those stupid trains? About those people staring out from the compartment windows, transient arrivals from strange, distant, indifferent places? For a few seconds they brought with them a hostile and rapacious atmosphere, smuggled into this sacred retreat the tumultuous hustle and bustle from their world, in stark contradiction of the spirit of the tunnel and its mysteries. And it always took a while for things to settle down after this brutal incursion, for the pockets of quiet and sweet slumbering to settle back into an even layer of tranquility . . .

Florek was fully aware of the fact that his very function as a tunnel guard was an inversion of the fundamental essence of this underground realm, that all of the actions he performed here ran counter to its most sacred ideals; he knew that he was serving 'those from above', facilitating their communication, sanctioning the crime of infiltrating the mysteries of Turbacz. He, a devotee of stony inertia, lover of silence and perpetual reverie, was looking after the safety of these intruders, destroyers of blessed peace, supporting their sacrilegious work by the labor of his own hands. Oh, the irony! . . .

His only solace in times of spiritual torment were his long, solitary strolls along the tunnel walls. He knew every projection, every recess, every fissure and rupture; even in the deepest darkness, he could orient himself by means of the 'level' of the wall at which he found himself. For the walls of the Turbacz tunnels had not been smoothed out in a uniform way. Having torn the guts of the mountain out to the width of a double railway line and thrown down dual ribbons of steel rails, they had left the walls almost in their natural state; they were consequently full of craters, faults, and bulges, jutting out toward the tracks at some points, receding at others into the bedrock.

Moisture seeped from the walls in places; secret, subsurface water from a spring somewhere deep within the rocks, emerging here and there upon the surface of the tunnel walls, flowed in narrow streams along cracks and crevices. At a particular point not far from the so-called 'Mole's Window' there gushed from the ribs of the rock a small waterfall which flowed out of the tunnel in the form of a crystal clear, ice-cold stream.

How delightful was this effusion from the stones of Turbacz! Dense, with a salty, sometimes limy taste, it draped across the rugged sections of the tunnel like a net of white saliva, hanging down in threads and tassels which opalesced with all the colors of the rainbow under the light of the electric lamps. Amid the underground silence, covered by the massive Turbacz peak, looming to a height of over 1900 meters, these cobwebs of water trickled with a barely perceptible murmur over the darkened rock ridges and moss-covered slabs. Florek would spend hours listening to the water's whispers, its drowsy prayers, pregnant with the slumber of the centuries. And there were moments when it seemed to him that he himself was that languid water, reciting his own drowsy prayers...

Then one day he made a strange discovery. He was sitting on one of the outcroppings of the Mole's Window, absorbed in the silence around him, when he suddenly felt that the boulder on which he was resting his feet wobbled and swayed. Curious, he slid off the rock above to examine the suspicious support and found that the boulder rocked in its foundation like a rotten tooth. He was able to push it over to the side, exposing a meter-wide crevice.

Undeterred by the absolute darkness of the place, Florek plunged into the black opening without hesitation. His peculiar eyes with their feline phosphorescence bored into the woolly darkness of the crevice and guided his path. He slithered between the cold, moisture-soaked stone walls like a snake, wriggled and slid his way through tight spots among the rocks like a salamander.

Suddenly his eyes were struck by a soft, bluish-green glow. The fissure widened, and he found himself standing in a broad cave bathed in this mysterious light. Where this pleasant illumination was coming from, he could not tell; the underground grotto appeared to be vaulted on all sides, with not the slightest opening to be discerned. It seemed that the rock comprising the walls of the cave possessed some kind of special chemical property that emitted this peculiar, soothing radiance.

From within, a silver-green stream flowed directly out from the virgin granite, cut a rivulet through the sand at the center of the cave and disappeared again under the rocks.

Above this stream, immersed in a flood of greenish light, there sat a figure, partially reclining: it looked like an old man with a strange, monstrous appearance. It was completely naked, with only a long, milky-white beard covering the front of its body all the way to the knees.

The figure's head was strangely shaped. Dramatically elongated towards the top of the skull and flattened at the sides, it did not give the impression of anything human. Where one would expect to find ears were only small, vestigial openings. It had no mouth, for what stood in for one could not be described as such; it was rather a wide-open slit with no sign of any teeth, lips, or gums. The old creature's arms which, by some singular caprice of nature, were fused to the sides of its body, appeared entirely useless. All that was left were the hands, with five fingers conjoined like a bat's wing by a membrane of flesh, ridiculous, splayed, with no freedom of movement, perpetually at hip level – more like flippers than hands.

The creature's most freakish physical anomaly was its legs. Fused together wholly from the thigh on down, they looked like the massive tail of a fish or amphibian, adapted for paddling in the watery element . . .

At the rustling of footsteps, the old thing twitched and turned its monstrous head toward the newcomer. Florek noticed then that the cave dweller had no eyes; there remained of them only a faint, vestigial trace in the form of two folds of skin like eyelid-slits below its brow. The monstrosity could not see him, but it could hear that he was there. Its flattened, half-animal face looked afraid. It retreated from the stream instinctively, into the depths of the cave.

Hoping to calm it down, Florek touched it gently on the arm. A shiver of fear ran through the cave creature's body, and a gibbering, throaty sound came from its chest. It was mute. To gain its trust, the guard took a piece of sugared bread from his pocket and held it to its mouth. The creature tasted it with the tip of its tongue and, after smacking its tongue on the roof of its mouth a few times, refused it with a movement of the head. But it must have understood Florek's friendly intention, for now it behaved more calmly and stopped trembling all over. Soon its flipper-like hand began to seek contact with the visitor. Although he felt strongly disgusted and repulsed, Florek offered his hand in greeting. Feeling a human hand in its fingers, the cave dweller trembled again. Its pale, sallow face took on a mixed expression of shame and embarrassment. But it did not let go of Florek's hand; in fact, it even seemed that it was trying to draw him closer to itself, as if it wanted to get a better idea of his appearance. For it began to make some heavy, clumsy movements with the help of its fused tail-legs, which enabled it to move its hand along Florek's body. It was evidently astonished by the result of this examination, for it lay motionless on one side for a while and gibbered something in an agitated fashion. Then the guard ventured a question:

'Who are you? What is your name? Where have you come from?'

It answered him with spasmodic movements of flippers and tail, and a few inarticulate sounds. Then it crawled to the edge of the stream and plunged one hand into its current. After a moment it took it out again and raised it up, and Florek observed with disgust that the old thing was clutching a long, fat worm in its fingers, which wriggled for a moment between the membranes of its fin until it disappeared into the open slit of its mouth.

The guard understood: this action was intended to explain the reason for its refusal of his friendly offer. The cave dweller ate only what the rocks and stream provided; human food was apparently no longer acceptable to it.

As Florek gazed pensively at his mysterious host, a pair of amphibians emerged from the water. They had roundish bodies twenty-five to thirty centimeters long, flesh-pink in color, with widely separated appendages, three in front and two in back, and a hairy tail with a fin. On both sides of their neck were the red slits of a triple gill and, under the thin, transparent skin of their heads one could discern two dots indicating a pair of eyes that had thoroughly wasted away. When they opened their little mouths slightly to suck in air, their tiny teeth shone in the green glow of the cave.

Having emerged from the water, the animals crawled over to the old creature, which began to run its hand with pleasure over their rounded bodies. They readily submitted to this caress, and it was apparent that they were accustomed to it, and that it was pleasing to them. At one point, the old one and the amphibians underwent the same strange alterations; their bodies suddenly began to take on various colors: the hitherto flesh-colored hue of their skin changed to whitish-pink, then to pink, then brown, then reddish-brown with dark spots, then finally returned to its original state. The phenomenon was singular and unusual; the man-creature and these amphibious beings seemed to be communicating through an interplay of flesh . . .

Lost in contemplation of the wonders of this strange, hidden place, Florek suddenly returned to his senses and looked instinctively at his watch. It was two minutes after midnight; a train would be passing through the tunnel in half an hour. He touched the old one's hand gently in farewell and quickly began to force his way back through the gap. A few minutes later he was restoring the tunnel to its normal, 'official' appearance and, squinting his eyes under the glare of the electric light, reassuming his official position in front of the guard's shed . . .

The discovery of the cave and its inhabitant had a decisive influence on Florek's life. From that moment on, he spent all his free time with this underground Proteus, whom he called 'Skalnik', or the rock-man. His duties as a railway guard fell to the level of a necessary evil, to which he paid tribute only grudgingly and with disgust.

On the other hand, he was fully alive in the company of the cave dweller and his amphibians. It was there that he found fulfillment of his desires, the safe haven he had always longed for. The Skalnik's cave became for him the 'Grotto of Oblivion'.

They continued to interact, becoming thoroughly accustomed to one another. During these regular meetings, they established a system of communication using signs, gestures, and sounds, allowing them to share information about themselves and their pasts. This is how Florek found out that his friend was a very old being; Skalnik calculated his own age at several hundred thousand years. But he could not give an exact number, as his memory had weakened and time had glided on before it like smoke, leaving no trace. Moreover, he had nothing to remember. He had passed centuries in the cave, centuries woven from gray days that were as similar to each other as the beads of a rosary. For all anyone could tell, he might have existed since primeval times, or from the time man uttered his first words on this planet . . .

He could only dimly recall that many, many centuries ago he had possessed a form similar to Florek's, but had renounced it in order to remain where he was. Others similar to him and Florek had moved forward at the cost of their lives – he had remained, breaking free from the dreaded hand of natural law; those others had submitted themselves to the injunction of a great sacrifice, to gain a new, higher form of life through death, then return to earth again, and in these new forms to ascend toward even greater heights – but he had fled from death, locking himself away from it in the 'Grotto of Oblivion' as though with iron bolts. There, outside, in the world, whirling with changes, in the frenzy of eternal movement, progenitor of life and death, young nations were budding, old and withered ones were being laid to rest, cultures and civilizations springing up, some rising, others falling into the abyss . . . Meanwhile, he endured forever and existed indifferent to everything, lonely, an outcast. Only his human body remained, though regressed to animalistic form, with his centuries-long contact with amphibians making him a bit more similar to them in his external features. But what did he care about that? Because he did not move forward, he renounced altogether the human right to eternal transformation and upward migration, he tore himself away from the embrace of death – he endured.

The cave-dweller was completely indifferent to the bustle of life in the outside world; he wasn't even interested in news from the other side that Florek brought him. He listened absently, preoccupied by something else, and when he again became attentive for a moment, he would shush Florek with a movement of his hand. Eventually Florek remained quiet and spoke no more about the people and the world outside.

Gradually, the 'Grotto of Oblivion' began to affect him down to his deepest self. For hours they sat, just the two of them, by the banks of the stream, gazing at its noiselessly rolling currents, listening to the great silence of the rocks. Sometimes, when the walls of the cave stopped phosphorescing, they were plunged into absolute darkness. These were the most beautiful moments. A great, stony reverie enveloped their souls so that they forgot about themselves, their own existence, and just persisted like the rocks surrounding them, without knowledge, without feeling, without thoughts. The eternal somnolence of the boulders flowed over them like a mysterious power and submerged them in a kind of stupor of forgetfulness – the terrible slumber of dead things paralyzed their arteries and petrified their blood with the solidity of rocky stagnation. The hoary, indolent spell of inertia cast its unctuous bonds upon them and chained them to the spot – the dual enchantment-bewitchment of the great mountains, the deadness of solidified immobility . . .

And they were like those ridge crests, that solid bedrock . . .

Until the time when a prolonged whistling broke through the silence of their secluded space. Florek roused, looked dumbfoundedly at his companion and pricked up his ears. The sharp, piercing sound tore through the interior of the mountain a second time, invading their solitude . . . The watchman jumped up as if horse-whipped and rushed through the crevice back into the tunnel.

There, in front of the guardhouse, the train was already waiting for him, enveloped in clouds of smoke and steam. Curious faces were staring from the compartment windows, conductors were walking nervously along the cars, and the traffic manager was jerking furiously at the handle of the locked guardhouse door. They were looking for him . . .

His heart pounding, Florek stood before his superior.

'Where have you been? Why were you away from your post again? Why is the tunnel so dimly lit?'

'I'm a few minutes late, sir,' mumbled the guard, semi-conscious. 'I was inspecting the track . . . I went too far towards the end of the tunnel and couldn't get back in time.'

'That's a lie! I've noticed your absence from the post a few times before. I will hold you accountable for this tardiness and dereliction of duty!' He turned to the engine driver and raised the trumpet to his lips. 'And now: Let's go!'

There rang out in response a tense call of departure; the locomotive let out a whistle and began rolling on . . .

Florek passed a sleepless night, leaning against the head of the stall.

At noon the next day, a special train carrying the criminal investigation committee arrived and suspended him from his post. Florek was ordered to leave the guardhouse immediately, which was then entrusted to the care of another officer brought in from a larger station.

When pleas for forgiveness and promises of improvement had no effect, the unfortunate watchman fell to his knees before the chairman of the commission.

'Mr. Inspector!' he begged in a whimpering voice. 'In the name of all that is holy! I beg you, sir, please let me stay here! I can't go! I won't leave the tunnel! . . .'

'We'll see about that, Mr. Florek, we'll see!' his superior responded coldly. 'We'll help you. Come on! Get him into a carriage! Under his arms! Quickly, now!' Several large, well-built men reached out to grab him.

'I beg you, gentlemen!' groaned the sorry fellow, retreating instinctively to the wall of the tunnel. 'Leave me here! Don't kill me!'

And he burst out crying like a child. The inspector snorted impatiently:

'No stupid scenes! We've no time for that. Gentlemen, do your duty!'

Arms reached out predatorily toward Florek. The watchman dodged them, coiled himself up like a snake and began to flee along the tunnel walls. By the time the stunned pursuers took stock of the situation, he was already on a beeline toward the Mole's Window. It was only then that they gave chase. Florek quickly skirted the stony outcropping, climbed up to the fissure and plunged into its mouth. Then, having sealed the opening with a massive block, he disappeared into the depths of the narrow chasm.

When his pursuers reached this spot a few seconds later, the fugitive had vanished without a trace. No one could guess that he had sunk into the rocks on the other side of the bend.

'Let's go, move it!' – the inspector encouraged his men. 'He seems to have gotten quite the jump on you. Where could he have gone? Maybe he's already made his way to the exit, or he's hiding somewhere in the shadows.'

'Why don't we get on the train and search through the tunnel with our torches?' one of them suggested. 'No use exhausting ourselves for no reason. A man is not a pin – you can't just lose him, and he can't sink into the ground. We'll track him down sooner or later.'

'Good idea!' his superior agreed. And they boarded the train, brightly lighting the way with their torches . . . But they did not track down Florek. Neither on that day, nor on the following days – never. He disappeared without a trace; like a stone in water, like a sound dissipating through space . . .

But since that time, rumors have circulated in the mountains that whenever Mother Earth undergoes some strong upheaval, and mankind falls into new ruts, there appear in the rocky chasms, in the blind ravines and mountainous passages, like an impotent resistance, or a futile warning, hoary monstrosities, half-animal, half-human, huge, dumb, blind things. And they call these old creatures the changelings of the cave . . .

Before a Long Journey

May 1905

A time of happiness and good cheer is beginning for me. Some good spirit has arrived at my doorstep, and grace is flowing into my household. My afternoons are now warm, heated by the sun, my evenings gentle, relaxing. My daytime labors are bearing fruit; I feel the respect of my peers, the love of my cherished wife. I am young, healthy, and strong. My arms flex with the manly energy of action, my brain readily solves the tasks set before it. I cross the street with a spring in my step, light, youthful, and carefree, feasting my eyes on the colorful variety of things. How beautiful, how fascinating the world is! . . .

My thirtieth year of life is off to a happy start. It promises to be a prosperous one, with good omens for the future. I am reaching the fulfillment of long-awaited goals; I stand in the world with a sure footing, calmly taking stock of the prospects unfolding before me. I am on my way to the summits marked out for me by my fate and abilities.

My dear friends bow their heads to me kindly to show their appreciation, unanimous in their esteem; the warm handshakes of strangers strengthen my conviction that I am not frittering away my life, but that I am important and needed here.

It seems that for some time now, perhaps even more so of late, significant changes have been taking place in my attitude towards life and its manifestations. I am beginning to perceive it in a more grounded way, with greater sincerity and passion. I have somehow become more intimate with the world, and with other people; I can distinctly sense the warm pulse of things around me. Life is beginning to have an entirely new charm for me, one I had never anticipated, as though its strange beauty has been somehow multiplied.

Each day I become a more devoted admirer of shapes and forms, of the elemental richness and variety of organic processes, and of the material side of life in general. I, once an advocate of ethereal abstractions, a creator of fictions dissipated by the slightest breath, today have come to love the physical and the concrete; I immerse myself with unhealthy delight even in everyday trivialities. There is a lyricism as deep as the sea hidden within it all, the melancholy love of something that is at once kind and hostile, charming and threatening, serious and at times as naïve as a child. Nowadays, I am strangely sympathetic and tender.

Winter 1905

I am finding myself more and more overwhelmed by an incomprehensible desire for amusement, an insatiable thirst for entertainment. I cannot sit still at home even for a moment. I have neglected almost all of my work in favor of having fun.

I have pulled Marta into this wild vortex as well. At first she put up a meek resistance, but over time she gave in, as she always tends to do with me. At times I have the impression that she looks at me fearfully, as if I were a madman, but because I'm always laughing at her unwitting fears, she ends up calming down and letting herself be carried away on the wave of excitement.

Among my circle of friends, I have apparently earned a reputation as a 'bon vivant', and as such, I never fail to show up at every soirée, charity event, or masquerade ball, to participate in sporting competitions, and to take the floor at boisterous gatherings. My lifestyle has even attracted the attention of the press. Whereas before, when I was very productive and serious about my work, they tried to ignore me with the typical 'deadly' silence, now they viciously attack me from all sides as if I were a beast of the apocalypse. They moralize constantly about my wasted talents, my general hellraising, my orgiastic mania and so on. I pay no attention to this and, from morning until late at night, and sometimes until the next morning, I party like a young buck.

And in my love life I have been consistently exceeding my prior limits. What's worse, I feel that I am downright abnormal. I think this is partly due to the hectic way of life I now lead. Some kind of primitive instincts have been awakened in me, along with a morbid excitability of the senses.

I only feel sorry for Marta. It is true that her character, which is as pliable as wax, quickly adapted to my changing desires, and not without a feeling of mutual delight; but even still, she is not enough for me now. It is terrible for me at times, but I cannot control myself. I am drunk. Fortunately, she knows nothing about this; she doesn't even harbor any suspicions. She would not put up with it. Yes, she has been especially good and understanding to me now. And yet . . . and yet, I am not happy.

In truth, there is nothing I lack, but nevertheless I feel somehow . . . strange. I have been experiencing moments of spiritual prostration and anxiety so suffocating that I jump out of bed at night and, slipping quietly out of the house, go off and drown my dark fears in various amusements. Something is choking me, strangling me. Sometimes I am afraid of my own shadow and do not dare to stay alone even for a few minutes.

I have to be continually around people, to see human faces, to hear human voices, to feel the presence of living beings. Even so, more and more often I find myself feeling terribly lonely, hopelessly isolated. Often, during the rowdiest of parties, when Marta's face, flushed with emotion, exudes that ineffable glow that I always admire so much in her, suddenly all the refined gentlemen in their tailcoats, all the elegant, effusively charming women – everything around me slips away as though into an immeasurable distance, and I am left on my own beneath the brash, enervating lights of the hall, alone, absolutely alone . . .

February 1906

They are all in unconscious agreement concerning me. Something like an *entente cordiale* has formed as to the attitude that should be adopted towards me.

How this came about exactly, I do not know; it developed

surreptitiously, but incontrovertibly. They themselves do not even realize what has happened, and if I were to ask them about it, everyone would certainly respond with bewilderment. And yet they are behaving quite differently towards me now than they did before. It's not an illusion – certainly not! There is something in it. It is not a question of scorn or condescension, quite the contrary. People are as polite to me as ever; even, I would say, obsequious, but – in this I've noticed a mysterious change that is consistent among everyone – their respect for me has become tinged with fear, a kind of elemental trepidation. It is not a reverential sort of fear, however, but something quite different . . .

What exactly is behind it all, I cannot tell.

All I have to go on are feelings and impressions. People behave towards me with anxious reserve. When I try to get closer, they instinctively shy away, albeit with every sign of respect. I know for certain that this does not stem from a sense of inferiority, or a desire to humble themselves – no, certainly not that. Rather, they regard me as something heterogeneous, irreconcilable with them, towards which a healthy instinct advises acting with caution. Sometimes I can't help but consider myself a foreign body among them.

My situation is all the more unbearable given the fact that I am presently more in need of human companionship than ever before. Meanwhile, wherever I appear, I immediately become a burden to those present. Naturally they dissimulate by covering the unpleasant feelings I evoke with a grimace of politeness, but I can see and feel them well enough, and I will not be deceived. It is abundantly clear that my presence makes them uneasy . . .

What makes it all the more strange is that I am usually in a crazy mood and try to amuse everyone in any way possible. And there are times when I succeed brilliantly; it is as though they forget everything, and a convivial desire flows warmly through their souls. But all it takes is a trivial detail, a slightly more serious remark made in passing, for everything to return to its former state, and that terrifying emptiness to surround me once again . . .

20 *February* 1906.

People I do not know have been coming up to me and speaking in riddles ... Signs appear, strange nods, and then, having played out their obscure roles before me, they slip away into the distance. Unusual events and ambiguous situations have been occurring which, having passed before my frightened eyes, dissolve into space ...

Something is going on around me! I can sense that something is about to happen ...

A few days ago I was with my wife at a masquerade. Marta aroused widespread interest with her gypsy costume. Throngs of masked faces perpetually circled her. I enjoyed myself like never before, clad in fisherman's garb with a green net slung over my shoulder. Safe under my mask, confident that I was incognito, I dished out jibes mercilessly, triggering bursts of laughter throughout the hall. No one guessed that the mischievously frolicking, madcap angler and the dark-haired gypsy were a married couple.

Nevertheless, in the midst of the most lively merriment, as the amused crowd literally tore us out of one another's arms, I had an odd and unpleasant encounter. At one point a tall, thin man in a domino approached me and remarked half-jokingly in passing:

'Merry fisherman, you cavort about like a madman, casting your net far and wide as if to catch all of us in it. But your net is empty; your catch slips through your hands, and the laughter which you so greedily solicit rings of insincerity. I can smell the water on you. You are saturated with the chill of the deep, and now you want to warm yourself here by violence. You give off the impression of a shadow desperate to become a solid object.'

I hurled myself at the impertinent fellow to give him a proper redressing, but he immediately disappeared among the crowd.

I was left with an exceedingly disagreeable impression. The stranger's cryptic words affected me deeply, unwittingly connected as they were with the mood I have been feeling of late. Only with Marta's untiring aid was I able to shake off the after-effects of this unpleasant episode, and we passed the rest of the night in good spirits.

1 *March* 1906.

For the past week now, I have been having the same dismal dream night after night. The same hopeless scene, obstinately repeating itself in all its dry monotony.

I find myself in a steep, dilapidated hallway with one partly shattered window looking onto the outside. A staircase ascends from the hallway, winding with a thousand turns, exhaustingly long . . . I'm standing on the first steps and slowly begin climbing the stairs. My feet plod along, treading heavily on the oak planks, stirring up deafening echoes in the empty space. The steps are filthy, coated in a thick layer of gray dust that rises in dark clouds under the impact of my footfalls, choking me. I can feel the dryness in the air and my tongue sticking to my palate. And the staircase winds interminably towards unseen floors, stretching inexorably upward with its banal succession of everyday objects. When I want to stop for a moment and take a look behind me, the ashen sea of steps flexes toward me in serpentine waves, so that I turn with trepidation from the gray abyss and climb onward, higher, using every ounce of my remaining strength, straining my frayed nerves. Beads of sweat appear on my forehead, cold as iron, my hands shake like crazy, and my dull gaze, focused on the possessed staircase, strays listlessly over the clusters of spiderwebs . . .

I walk like this for hours, without a break, all night long, and when silvery dawn peeks into my bedroom, I awake feeling brutally exhausted, weary as a pilgrim. A gray and dismal dream . . .

6 *March*.

I am still being tormented by the same nightmare. For the second week in a row now, every night I find myself walking up the filthy staircase, swallowing the dust of its decayed steps. But certain changes have occurred. The dream seems to be developing new motifs and moving toward some sort of resolution . . .

I am no longer alone on the dusty stairs; I have a companion. I've been encountering him since last Saturday, always more or less at the midway point of the ascent. He seems to be the caretaker of this strange house, because a set of old, rusty keys clank together in his hand. He comes down from somewhere on the upper floors, walking so quietly that you can't hear his steps; he moves along the stairs like a shadow.

A peculiar fellow. He never looks at me, as though he is afraid of my gaze, but warily moves his elongated figure close to the wall to get out of my way. I endeavored several times to look him in the face, but his broad felt hat, drawn low over his forehead, thwarted my efforts.

Having passed me, he descends further and disappears abruptly like a phantom, while I fiercely, breathlessly continue climbing toward higher and higher floors . . .

Only yesterday did I finally reach the end of this mad staircase, where I found myself standing on a square platform before a set of wrought-iron doors . . .

Exhausted, I leaned against the rotted balustrade of the last staircase opposite the large double doors and stared at the iron crossbars . . . What if I were to open them and look inside?

I pounded against their iron surface with all my might, but only managed to bloody my hands, which became cramped from the pain and fell limply at my sides.

Undaunted, I pressed my whole weight against the doors, trying to break them off their hinges, and struggled with the stubborn bolts in hopes of tearing them from their rivets. But the bonds held with relentless obstinacy and would not yield to my efforts.

When I was about to fall to my knees in discouragement, I felt someone slip a sharp steel tool into my hand. I took hold of it with elation, realizing that this would make my task easier, and turned towards my unexpected helper in gratitude. But all at once, I jumped back frantically into the corner between the wall and the balustrades. The man who wanted to do me a favor was the 'care-taker' I had been meeting on my way up the stairs. The hat did not conceal his face now – ha, ha! – there was no face to conceal, for in its place there gaped a pair of empty black pits! . . .

10 *March.*

It seems to me that I have dreamt my dream through to the end. The scene that I witnessed tonight bears all the hallmarks of an epilogue. If it comes to pass tomorrow, those sober-minded observers of life who have been monitoring my debauched activities with astonishment will perhaps finally understand them and, no longer regarding me as a lunatic, will bow their heads in reflection:

'This is the way it had to be.'

I write these words calmly; so calmly that at times I am surprised at myself. And yet – tomorrow!

The hours pass in their usual way, tolled out at regular intervals by the old clocks; the activities of the day repeat themselves with the indifferent regularity of ordinary things.

Outwardly, nothing is happening. Everything is just as it was before, with nary a suspicious crack or concerning alteration to be found. How strange, how terribly strange! Even so – tomorrow!

Although . . . perhaps I am wrong to take the creations of a sick brain seriously, perhaps I am wrong . . . In any case, I do not care; I am so apathetic, so submissively resigned . . .

Actually, I do not even know why I am writing this. The value of these few pages hinges on what happens tomorrow; if it answers to the dream, this diary will prove an interesting document.

I seem calm, but my whole body is shivering as though with fever, and I can hardly focus on jotting down these lines. I must hurry, moreover, because I have very little time today and I would like to visit all my friends . . .

I would like now to recount tonight's epilogue, the end of the dream that has been tormenting me for weeks. A truly stylish finale! . . .

At some point during the night, I found myself again before the wrought-iron doors. They stood as inexorably closed off as they had last time. But upon closely examining one of them, I noticed a rectangular hole cut out of it. I had probably carved it myself with a file the night before, though I couldn't recall the relevant image in my dream.

I looked through the opening.

Behind the door was a room.

It looked like the study of a well-to-do gentleman, decorated with taste and exquisite simplicity.

In a corner stood a glass-fronted walnut bookcase, in the middle a desk, next to it a small table with chairs upholstered in dark green leather. On the walls were a few paintings whose subjects I do not remember.

Behind the desk, a man was sitting in a broad armchair with his back turned to me, writing something. From time to time he would put down his pen to take a drag on a cigar that was smoking in the ashtray beside him, before returning assiduously to his work. And it was odd, the way he worked.

The stranger was evidently not writing a continuous piece of text, for every few moments he would set aside a rapidly dashed-off page and replace it with a fresh one. I had the impression that he was busy addressing letters. I tried to catch a glimpse of his features, but I could not: he remained sitting with his back to the opening, and did not so much as turn around once.

Meanwhile, next to him on the desk, a stack of cards was steadily piling up. They were folded in half, made of stiff, shiny cardboard, and each had four lines in freshly printed ink on the back side. They were obviously various people's addresses.

From this I deduced that the cardboard envelopes must contain some kind of printed content, and that it must be the same for everyone: invitations to some family celebration, perhaps?

Suddenly he stopped writing, rubbed his forehead and, as if remembering something, pressed the button to summon the servant.

The servant came in. The master, without leaving his seat, gave some order accentuated by a gesture and then, hiding his face in his hands, leaned his elbows on the desk and seemed to be thinking . . .

Just then, a set of doors opposite opened and several men entered carrying an oblong, cylindrical bundle; two young men followed behind, bringing three folding ladders into the room.

The master of the house did not raise his head, but continued sitting motionlessly in his former position.

Then the men began to unroll the bundle, from which broad,

moiréed sheets of shiny black taffeta slid to the floor. One of the young men positioned the ladder against the wall of the study and, nodding to his companion, slipped quietly out of the room. The others divided themselves into pairs; one partner ascended the rungs, hoisting the raven-black fabric up with him, while the other, remaining at the bottom, unfurled the roll and used scissors to cut the material once it reached the appropriate length to cover the wall.

Next, the mourning crepe was nailed into place. I could clearly hear the dull clatter of hammers striking the wall, and the harsh sound of nails penetrating the hard surface grated on my ears . . .

The work proceeded at a frantic pace; after only a short time the horrible tapestries were hung all around, covering everything in a uniform, shiny metallic black.

Upon finishing, the workers departed. The stranger still sat motionless at his desk, not raising his face. He did not seem to notice the change his surroundings had undergone.

Then the opposite door opened again and some boys came in with vases full of flowers, large pots with fresh bunches of tuber-oses, carnations, and myrtles, along with a stack of wreaths with white sashes. They placed all of these by the window and went out.

Shortly after, a servant appeared at the entrance, opened the double doors wide and gestured for others to enter. Only then did the master of the house stand up, in order to receive the guests. Leaning with his left hand on the edge of the table, he extended his other hand in a refined gesture of welcome.

He did not wait long; presently a group of male figures in black evening dress appeared in the doorway. Quickly walking across the runner which had been spread from the entrance to the desk, they silently shook hands with their host. Their faces were solemn, stern, focused. I recognized them; they were my closest acquaint-ances. Others began to enter. None of them were strangers to me: co-workers, colleagues, people I had met casually at one place or another. Among the dense crowd of people clad in evening dress, I spotted here and there a few women from the society to which I belonged.

The guests, having greeted the master of the house, filed further into the room, gradually filling it with a dark throng. No conversations nor even whispering could be heard: a deafening silence reigned, not even broken by words of greeting; hands were only extended and shaken without words, as if in silent agreement . . .

Suddenly the crowd parted amidst signs of deference and, forming two parallel rows, let a woman dressed in heavy mourning robes pass between them. From beneath a disheveled veil spilled locks of dark blonde hair which shimmered with a warm glow; slender and limber as a reed, she walked with a step full of latent gentility, which even the pain and grief of the moment could not erase.

On seeing her enter, the stranger approached her with open arms. She slipped between them without a word and rested for a time in his silent embrace. After a while, he raised her up by her slender waist and, supporting her on his arm, pulled the veil away from her eyes . . . The woman was my wife . . .

For a long, long time he gazed at her face, into her beautiful eyes, taking in the sweetness of her visage. Then slowly, without taking his eyes off her, he reached a hand back towards the desk, removed one of the cards from the stack, opened it and gave it to Marta to read . . .

It was a funeral announcement. The date caught my attention: March 11, 1906, and above it the name of the deceased: Atosal. A strange name! . . .

It suddenly occurred to me that it should be read backwards . . . I began to do so . . . As I worked out the letters in reverse, the stranger slowly turned to face me and . . . I awoke to my own screams of terror . . .

Annotation by the diary's publisher:

> *W. Lasota died suddenly on March 11, 1906,*
> *struck on the head by a brick falling from a scaffold.*

Blind Man's Buff

Grześ Lutomski was passionately fond of Blind Man's Buff. This simple, uncomplicated game had a special charm whose essence it would have been difficult for him to put into words. It was made up of various intangible elements bound together into a whole that was strangely beautiful and enchanting.

There was something mysterious about the game, something that eluded the controlling grasp of definitions – unusual, peculiar, enigmatic . . .

He sometimes wondered who came up with the game. Father claimed that it was very old and had been known among children since time immemorial. Grześ's mother, a beautiful, black-haired woman with a slightly melancholy cast to her large, dark eyes, supposed with a slight smile at the corners of her mouth that the game had been invented in a fit of boredom by an Arabian prince who lived centuries ago, when he got sick of looking at the world and its hypocrisy.

'In any case,' thought Grześ, 'it must have been someone very remarkable and clever.' Children had enjoyed the game for so many centuries without tiring of it, and some, among them Grześ Lutomski, preferred it over any other game. And quite rightly so. All one had to do was consider how the game started: that magnificent action of blinding the eyes with a handkerchief. Magnificent, even supremely so, but only if the handkerchief is tied carefully and securely; not, it should go without saying, the way that little brat Zbych Raduski does it, leaving a little 'chink' at the bottom, which is against the rules. Of course, that's not true Blind Man's Buff, just a common cheat, which always irritated Grześ immensely. After all, the whole appeal of the game comes from the fact that you can't see anything at all and have to search in total darkness.

It was precisely this voluntary blindness, this temporary closing of the eyes to one's surroundings, that marked a moment of
profound strangeness for him. It always seemed to Grześ that he
had passed suddenly into an unknown world, one wonderfully
alien and full of surprises. While the hushed steps of his playmates
slipping past him and the muffled laughter of those who managed
to dodge and lure him in the wrong direction confirmed that
there existed a primary world, lately abandoned, right beside
him, Grześ nevertheless felt in these moments a net of mystery
stretched around him, subtle and elusive, yet strong as steel. And
like a swimmer in water, he would plunge with his arms gleefully
outstretched into its mysterious depths.

'Uh-oh! Grześ is rowing again!' mocking voices would yell
from the corners of the room.

'His arms are waving like windmill blades!' teased a shrill, girlish voice.

'Swim, blind man, swim on the stormy stream of life!'[1] sang
Zbych Raduski in an imitation bass, his voice already cracking.

And Grześ swam. Buttoned up in his tight school uniform and
blindfolded, with his brow creased and his arms flailing in space, he
looked like a symbol of humanity striving amid adversity. He cared
little whether he caught anyone from among the apprehensive
group, and sometimes voluntarily let go of a captured victim. Like
a player of the highest caliber, he despised cheap and easy prizes.

'Lutomski, he's a first-rate sportsman,' was what Janek Przegocki, only sixteen but already a big lout, used to say. 'He passes
up the small fish that carelessly wander too close and only hunts for
larger game.'

'You may well be right,' Grześ would answer coldly, before
'swimming off' in the opposite direction.

And when, after several minutes of searching, he tired of the
effort and decided to catch someone 'for real', he succeeded almost
instantly; like a wildcat ready to pounce, he would suddenly exe-
cute a surprise turn and catch someone with a single swipe of his
arm, usually the one who least expected it. He would then remove
the blindfold and return among the people.

1 A line from *Pieśń żeglarów* (Sailors' Song) by E. Wasilewski. [Translator's note.]

Raduszki was always struck by the expression on his face at such moments.

'You know, Grześ,' he once said at the close of a game, 'you always look a little weird after Blind Man's Buff, as if you were not the same somehow. Like you just woke up from a deep sleep, or . . .'

'Or what?'

'Hm . . . I don't know. How can I say it? Like you just fell back to earth from the moon. Ha, ha, ha! And you're not sure what to do with yourself among earthlings! Really – that's the impression I get.'

'Perhaps that's an accurate observation,' Grześ muttered, looking thoughtful.

And yet everyone agreed that without him there could be no 'true' Blind Man's Buff. He was the soul of the game, the one who elevated it to a higher level and, by virtue of his behavior, imparted to it a rather singular and unusual quality. He was the unwitting axis around which the game turned, toward which all of the players' attention was drawn, and toward which they gravitated in a way that was unmistakable yet mysterious. This was shown also by the fact that the children considered it an honor and a distinction if he deigned to catch one of them during the game. There was no doubt about it: Grześ Lutomski was the unrivaled master of Blind Man's Buff.

This was true of him not only in the role of seeker. Likewise, among the skittish crowd of those avoiding the seeker, he always came to the fore, yet never allowed himself to be caught. Thanks to an almost superhuman dexterity, he always managed to slip away right at the most critical moments. He would flit away like an eel just as the blind man's hand was nearing, or slither just off to the side like a snake, moving away scot-free almost right behind the seeker's back. There was no spot so tight that he couldn't find some means of squeezing his way out of it.

And yet, one could never accuse him of being overly cautious. Quite the contrary. He was constantly in the line of fire, always at the forefront, ceaselessly taunting, misleading, and disorienting the blind man. And sometimes it happened that, quietly as a ghost, he would proceed half a step in front of him, just a short distance from his outstretched arm, or accompany him for minutes at a time just behind his back, so close as almost to be brushing against it.

How he managed to attain such mastery of the game, no one could tell; it was his secret. In general, however, he decidedly preferred the role of blind man and gladly allowed himself to be blindfolded.

Over time, the game became a passion that grew visibly with each passing day, until the boy got drunk on it like wine. Desiring complete freedom of movement, he worked gradually to convince his parents to allow him a suitable spot for the game. Finally they gave him the biggest room in the apartment, hitherto known as the 'drawing room', and agreed without reservation to any 'changes' Grześ saw fit to make within it. Soon after, by his orders, the room was completely emptied; every last piece of furniture was removed, so that an unpleasant vacuity reigned between the four walls, and an echo rumbled dully, roused from its slumber. It was here in this cleared space that, two afternoons a week, the most ardent devotees of Blind Man's Buff gathered.

The game usually began around five o'clock and continued, with breaks, until evening. As a prelude, an 'arch-seeker' was elected, whose responsibility was to direct the game, hand out penalties for any rule violations, and settle any disputes that might arise among players.

Of course, this important post was most often entrusted to Grześ, who fulfilled its duties with the utmost diligence. Everyone therefore agreed with his verdicts without so much as a murmur of dissent, and no one ever questioned his impartiality. Even in the most difficult cases, namely when Grześ himself was the blind man and therefore had no direct control over the game for some time, there were no disputes, and no doubts raised.

Lutomski remained in control of the situation even in times of 'blindedness'. And yet, after a while he began to lose some of his former confidence in this regard and would find himself hesitating.

When, on one particular occasion, tired of playing the seeker, he decided to 'really' catch someone and so executed one of his extraordinary half-turns to the right, he succumbed to some kind

of mistake or delusion he'd never before experienced. Extending his hand in that direction, he expected to seize hold of Zosia
Szadurska, who had for some time been daring to tap him on the
shoulder from behind – but instead his fingers encountered some
kind of hard, sharp-angled object, with a texture like wood or
cardboard. Startled, he quickly snatched off his blindfold, but to
his astonishment saw nothing before him except his own clenched
fist. He became enraged; someone was making a fool of him.

'Who the devil put a piece of wood or cardboard in front of
me?' he asked, glaring menacingly at the group around him.

There was a moment of silence, and then everyone broke out in
laughter. Of course, no one admitted guilt.

'He's messed up, for once! Hurrah!'

'Uh-oh, something's rotten in Denmark!'

Their expressions and exclamations seemed sincere; he decided
that they were not lying. He bit his lip angrily and fell silent, placing the blindfold back over his eyes.

Even worse blunders were to follow. Once he thought he had
caught someone's arm in passing, but upon removing his 'blinder'
found that the space between his clenched fingers was empty.

'What the devil?' he thought. 'Could they really have slipped
away so fast?'

But he quickly dismissed this notion as not holding up to
scrutiny. Surely he would have felt someone slipping out of his
grasp, but there had been no sensation of something being yanked
away. He had plainly felt someone's arm under his fingers, yet in
the next second this impression was completely gone. And that
was it. Moreover, the arm was muscular and veiny, something of
which none of his playmates could boast – not even Jan Przegocki
himself. No – it was the arm of a grown man!

Having learned from these two strange experiences, Grześ
began to keep quiet about his sensations during the game, and to
play more carefully; he now preferred not to let go of his quarry,
rather than fool around by proclaiming an imaginary triumph
over himself. Meanwhile, the puzzling impressions grew more
frequent. In nearly every game he came up against some unknown
thing, rubbed his fingers over some strange, peculiar or unusual

object. It might be something stiff, with bizarre contours, or the warm, pulsating arm of some kind of furry creature, but he also encountered what were clearly human figures. Sometimes while searching he felt the cool breeze of a shawl fluttering by, other times he detected someone's muffled whisper, or the echo of a sigh . . .

These impressions aroused in him a simultaneous fear and delight. Thus for months he dwelt as though in an enchanted garden, full of strange and wonderful things. Gradually life began to lose all appeal for him beyond the confines of the game, which had opened him up to a new world, a realm of enchantment and mystery. He spent hours doing nothing but daydream about those brief, all-too-fleeting moments that allowed him to venture into his beloved land. At last, driven by this uncontrollable longing, he decided to wander on his own into this enticing labyrinth. And so one afternoon, instead of waiting for Thursday's scheduled game, he locked himself up alone in the empty room.

It was five o'clock, and the room was saturated in summer warmth. All was silent in the house, with no one in any of the adjacent rooms. A ray of July sunlight crept through the closed window, leaving a golden trail across the floor . . .

Blindfold in hand, Grześ stood in the center of the room. He felt somehow uncomfortable; slowing his breathing, he listened to the pounding rhythm of his own heart, which was beating forcefully, in a state of alarm. For some reason he felt as though he were committing a shameful act, something that no one else should know about.

He looked around at the walls. They stared back with cold emptiness. Indifference. The only sound was that of a small branch from the viburnum bush outside, tapping against the sun-drenched windowpane . . .

Grześ pulled himself together, placed the blindfold over his eyes and secured it tightly. His solitary game began. As usual, he stretched his arms out in front of him, leaned forward a bit and began to 'search'.

At first, he found the loneliness intimidating; the utter silence, with no playmates whispering around him, and the complete certainty that there was not a single living soul in the room had a depressing effect. Gradually, however, he got used to it and, forgetting all about his surroundings, became completely absorbed in the act of searching. With trembling hands, he tore through space like a water polyp breaking apart mineral deposits with its tentacles – he swept aside invisible waves with the motion of his arms, elastic as eels ... Nothing. Only eddies of air violently cut by the movement of his own hands or the tramping of his feet on the floor.

Drops of sweat accumulated on his forehead and trickled down in warm streams over his cheeks.

He continued searching. At one point he carelessly struck his head against a wall, and then he badly injured his elbow. He didn't notice this and felt no pain. Half-conscious, like a dervish possessed in a frenzied dance, he continued circling the empty room ...

Suddenly he trembled. Something had awoken; having lain dormant in the surrounding space, this mysterious thing was now roused from the numbness of sleep. Currents began to flow, quiet, penetrating streams that began to pass through him. Someone touched him once, then again – someone lifted him up for a second ...

Who is that? Grab him! Stop him! Clench this elusive creature tightly in your fist! Oh-ho! I've got you at last! You won't escape like water through my fingers now!

Something thumped its chest hard up against his, and Grześ immediately closed his arms around it, wrapping the figure in a steel embrace.

'You won't get away, little bird, not again!' he said, laughing in wild triumph. He tightened his left arm around his quarry, and with his right hand tore the blindfold from his eyes.

Then he saw in the empty space of the room, as though suspended in the air a few inches from his own face, the face of another: a young, handsome boy of about fourteen. The face seemed familiar, as though he had seen it before in some mirror. Then at once he understood, and with a shudder of horror he jumped backward: it was his own face ...

And then it underwent a peculiar transformation: the soft,

boyish features hardened, became sharp, and the gentle blue eyes took on a steely sheen; the stern, implacable mask now fixed him with a hawklike glare.

Grześ screamed, cowering in the corner of the room. Then the apparition smiled. It was a singular smile – one of fatherly forbearance, understanding, and irony all at once . . .

It dawned like a brief flash of light upon a cloud, and went out. The vision dissipated in space . . .

When the Lutomskis returned home a quarter of an hour later, they entered the empty room and found Grześ clutching his blindfold in his hand, staring blankly at the opposite wall.

'What's the matter, son?' his mother asked, concerned.

'Nothing, it's nothing. Foolishness,' he said, shaking off his bewilderment. 'I was just imagining things.'

He preferred not to give a more detailed explanation. But from that day on, he never allowed himself to be blindfolded again.

Orchard of the Dead

There is peace here; peace, and perpetual quiet. The song of the passer-by who happens to stray here in his wanderings soon falls silent. Even the birds cry more softly here . . .

Birches and guelder-roses tilt their heads somberly over the weatherbeaten walls, overgrown with moss and weeds, expressing the longing of the interior to the world outside. For everything here abides in sorrowful reverie.

The sand-covered paths wind off into the distance, separating the rows of graves beneath the crosses. Sadness reposes in the shade, spinning the gentle yarn of fates now fulfilled . . .

In the air, a powerful aroma. It comes from the scented lindens and acacias, flows from apple and pear trees. A robust, hearty aroma.

Trees are plentiful in this cemetery orchard, and shrubs of varieties too numerous to count. Apple trees buckle under their crop, pear trees glisten in ruddy abundance, plum trees stand amidst the deep purple of their fruits. An orchard and a cemetery at once . . .

From a thicket of wild roses protrude the black arms of a cross, conjuring up melancholy thoughts; these will be dispersed by the wind when, having glanced against a cherry tree in passing, it conceals this symbol of death with a branch laden with succulent fruit. And again the orchard basks in its own reddish glow . . .

There beneath a sycamore stands a woman; she has thrown a stone shawl over her downcast head in a gesture of profound agony, and is weeping . . .

Do not stare! She is a sepulchral mourner. There, to her left, the apple trees are greeting the smiling sweet-cherries with a sweeping bow . . .

From under the mossy stalks of burdock a torso protrudes,

half consumed by the air. A grave angel, no doubt, who once had guarded the deceased – now it rests, weary, no longer fulfilling its duty. May it sleep in peace and tranquility!

Among the clumps of mullein, the blackened remnants of an old cross rot away, eaten by worms. Clusters of hepatica flowers gush out from some corner. Life proliferates from the humus of the subsoil . . .

Gilded grave plaques shimmer in the glare of the autumn sun; desiccated wreaths and black-beaded rosaries droop from headstones. The abundant produce of the earth has come to rival the brilliant flood of rays from above, for it has grown rich – smells of mint and chamomile waft up, yellow petals of St. John's wort spread open, the smooth leaves of strawflower plants gleam whitely . . .

It is quiet here in this cemetery orchard, quiet and forlorn. At times the silence is broken by the thud of an apple falling from a tree, the buzzing of a bee circling a flower, the soft chirping of a bird . . . The shadows of the tree trunks move slowly, marking noonday in the life of the dead . . .

A gray-haired old man walks along a thistle-choked path, holding a young girl by the hand. A profound and quiet joy radiates from their eyes as they step among the graves. The man's kindly, faded eyes are smiling, and the girl's face shines with happiness. The man is Gregor, the cemetery keeper, and the girl his granddaughter.

Many years ago, after losing his young wife while in the prime of his life, he likewise lost his taste for farming and became a gravedigger. At first he only buried townsfolk, then he began to give final services to villagers also. Old Gregor's fate was a sad one. He outlived everyone in his family.

He had buried his wife, his mother, and his daughter – only his beloved granddaughter remained, for whose life he had prayed fervently to the dead.

For once a great plague had befallen the children of the village, and there was no hut or house from which weeping could not be heard. For two weeks, that rosy-lipped maiden walked among the homesteads and houses, stopping before the windows and spreading open her roughspun spotted shawls. Any child who offered her its hand fell like a flower cut down by a sickle. Gregor trembled with fear lest the pest-maiden also gather up his beloved Magda, the only one left to him in the world, into her shawls. Therefore, whenever he buried one of the victims, he made them a vow that he would walk like a father around their graves if they would beg the Lord to spare his granddaughter.

Eventually the plague subsided, and Magda remained among the living.

Having buried the final child, the old man gave up his woeful occupation forever and settled down with his granddaughter in the 'cemetery of the innocents'. This is what people called the place situated between the village and the town, where the victims of this terrible disease were buried separately, far from the former cemetery. Afterwards, no more bodies were laid to rest here; the burial ground was surrounded by a wall and locked up.

The former gravedigger lived within, inside the wooden building that had formerly served as the mortuary, and looked after the cemetery. He quickly became accustomed to the place, and soon found himself deeply attached to it.

Mindful of his promise, he tended to this poor neglected place as he had once tended his own fields. He set right the graves, topped up the soil, and straightened the crooked crosses.

And Magda was grateful to the dead for her gift of life. She planted flowers and herbs on the graves, wove wreaths, and weeded the overgrown paths. The gravedigger's granddaughter liked the melancholy place and the long, deep reveries it conjured. She knew all the children who lay here under the ground in their small white coffins; she was in the habit of talking to them often when, lying on the grass, she would rest her sleepy head under their cross.

And there were children from all walks of life. There were children of the town's wealthiest residents, used to abundance during their lives, clad in elegant dress – and there were poor ones from the backstreets, smoky huts without chimneys, perpetually hungry and ragged, their white teeth chattering with cold, buried in only a shirt because it was all their mothers could afford. Beside ornate marble monuments, lachrymal urns, and stone angels with snow-covered wings sat simple wooden crosses, huddling in the shade of the guelder-rose trees.

Magda loved them all equally, holding each one likewise close to her heart, united by a common fate . . .

Meanwhile, the cemetery was changing, becoming strangely more beautiful with the passage of years.

Gradually, Gregor transformed it into an orchard. He planted apple trees, pear trees, cherry trees, and plum trees, one on every little grave, and watched them like a hawk, protecting them throughout the winter.

And one autumn several years later, Magda approached her grandfather with a beautiful, blushing apple as big as a fist.

But the old man, though no doubt pleased with the harvest, reprimanded her sternly and forbade her from plucking the grave-yard fruit.

'You must not! It is theirs, the fruit of those who died.'

Magda became sad and, looking at Gregor with all the profundity of her deep black eyes, asked:

'But why, grandfather? What good are apples or pears to them? Are they really such bad dead children? After all, you have often said yourself that those on the other side are better than we who are alive, because death has already cleansed them of their sins.'

Gregor delighted in the girl's simple words.

'I did, because it is true; but, you see, a kind of fear grips me whenever I reach for one of those fruits. I feel as though I am stealing from them. All of their joy has sprung forth from their own ashes. For their time in this world was so brief they scarcely tasted even the slightest crumb of happiness, cut down at the dawn of their lives by greedy death. Look how many little girls, how many would-be maidens sleep there in silence, not having lived out their years. Each of them could have one day grown up to be a spirited young lady, comely and robust, and to get married and live happily with her husband, leaving a nice cottage behind for their children . . . But God did not grant it. Things turned out dif-ferently. Let them at least now delight in what has shot up from their decaying bones, let at least these traces of them remain. This is why I prefer to leave the fruit alone. It is theirs, it has blossomed from their bodies, and so let it return to them. It is not good to touch the fruits of the dead.'

And so the matter rested.

In the spring, the orchard wore a flowery gown of pale pink apple-tree petals, snowed over with the fluffy down of cherry and pear blossoms; over the summer, it matured amid the sun's kisses; in the autumn, it gave forth a yield of firm and succulent fruits. And when spiders began to weave their silvery webs against the pale sky, and autumn roses were wound about the gardens, a dense haul of round apples and pears as slender as bellflowers fell to the ground, to lie in the grass among the dark purple plums.

No one disturbed them; everything lay untouched in its abundant surplus like the bounty of grace, rich but despised. And when they were about to rot, and bruises began to blight their smooth faces, Gregor would wrap them in a sheet and bury them in the graves, returning them from whence they came.

There was just a single, paltry apple tree growing by itself near the mortuary building from which the cemetery keeper dared to pick fruit for himself and his grandchildren. This tree grew far from the graves and had no contact with the bodies of the deceased.

'This here is my only compensation, what these poor creatures give me for my service. I trust they would not begrudge me the fruits of this one tree.'

The rest of the trees bore generously, but in vain, for the produce was left unused. Neither the villagers nor the townsfolk dared to remove anything from the orchard, in holy fear of retribution from the dead. And on the odd occasion that some impudent scoundrel picked a fruit through the wall while passing by, people said that he regretted it bitterly afterwards; either he came down with a horrible disease, or was gripped by terrors during the night, or suffered some even more grievous misfortune.

At least, such were the rumors. But Magda did not put much stock in them.

'Just people being people!' she would often respond to Gregor whenever he cryptically repeated those rumors. 'They talk nonsense and make things up about those who don't buy into their ravings. But I stand behind my convictions. The dead are better than you say, not greedy for their apples and pears.'

The old man smiled, nodding his head as if in agreement, but still he acted the same way each year.

And so the cemetery continued to bear fruit, exerting itself year after year in this act of creative toil, only for this produce to be consigned uneaten back to the earth below. Only bluebirds and worms were left to nibble at the colorful swathes of fruit strewn among the grass and weeds, boring small holes into the pulp before abandoning the rest, leaving it to rot away.

Over time the orchard seemed to grow tired of this pointless production and began to give forth increasingly scantier yields. It became harder to spot an apple or pear in the red bloom of health amid the riotous greenery, and the purplish carpet of plums grew ever more threadbare. These shunned gifts from the grave now hid below the surface as if in shame, unwilling to emerge from the darkness.

Only the apple tree near the mortuary, which Gregor and his granddaughter used, bore fruit as it always had, and now even more generously. Surely no finer apples could be found in the whole region. They were as big as a child's head, juicy yet somehow oddly crumbly at the same time.

How could this be, when it seemed the rest of the trees were growing barren? The cemetery keeper was deeply troubled by this and racked his brain for a reason. He would gladly have given his soul to remedy the disaster. So he tilled the ground and fertilized it with fresh manure and rich black soil – all in vain: the following autumn, only a few straggling apples and pears could be spotted, dangling alone on the somber trees.

And so the old cemetery grew quieter and more gloomy. In the past, it used to be that orioles, blackbirds, and ash-gray larks, attracted by the ruddy fruits among the foliage, would swarm down among the graves and chirp all day long, into the night. In the spring, worker bees lured by the tempting scent of honey would descend on transparent wings with their silvery buzz, plant their eager tongues in the whorls of the petals and suck from the apple and cherry blossoms. Now they flitted by indifferently, gliding on to the meadows where a more sumptuous feast awaited.

There was only the song of Magda wandering among the sleeping graves to break the silence of this lonely place. She hummed melodies of longing infused with the quiet sorrow of the orchard; they trembled with regret for hopes unfulfilled, and the pain of happiness swept away, cut down in the middle of its course. She was the sentient soul of the cemetery orchard and of those who rested there. She knew her dead by name, and for each of them she cherished a doleful remembrance. Under her loving hand, the children's graves were colored with rose and jasmine bushes and fringed with creeping clusters of sedum.

But above her, the trees stood sparsely speckled with fruit. Sorrow gripped Magda's good heart at the memory of that autumn when they had been graced with a rich harvest, and she had first brought her grandfather that especially ripe and juicy apple. Crestfallen, she spent her evenings sitting on a bench beneath a chestnut tree, or wandering the white paths in deep reflection. The autumn sun would sift its golden dust through the sieve of foliage, flowing down in a slanted wave onto her dark head, framing her in a scarlet halo . . . Long shadows extending from the tree trunks would settle in a long row at the base of the walls, while the evening wind murmured softly among the latticework of branches, crickets chirped timidly, and dewdrops sprinkled softly from heaven to earth . . .

It was on just such an evening that Magda dared to do what she had contemplated for a long time, but had not yet done for fear of Gregor. She took advantage of a moment when the old man was chopping wood and smoking his pipe behind the cottage to approach the pear tree growing over little Marysia's grave, once so abundant and now nearly wasted away, and bravely plucked one of the fruits. Then she hurried off between the gooseberry bushes, dived down into the grass at the other side of the orchard and, with long-awaited delight, consumed the sweet, lusciously juicy pear.

When she returned to the cottage at night and went to sleep, she had a strange dream.

It seemed to her that, around midnight, a little girl sat down at the foot of her bed and gazed at her with deep blue eyes, hands working to untangle the flaxen braids in her hair. Magda wanted to ask her something, but the little girl, smiling, put her finger on her lips and, nodding her head as if in gratitude, kissed her on the mouth and went away.

And Gregor's granddaughter recognized the girl as Marysia, daughter of a poor widow, who had died years earlier during the plague.

At first she was very much afraid that the deceased had come to reclaim the fruit she had picked from the tree, but her smile, tender and full of gratitude, and the kiss with which she said goodbye to Magda, dispelled her fear.

The next morning, immediately after waking, she ran with a fluttering heart into the orchard, to Marysia's pear tree. And there she saw a curious thing: on the branch from which she had plucked yesterday's pear now hung two other pears, freshly grown overnight, golden, shapely as teapots, and shining as though iced with a yellow glaze.

A current of profound joy flowed warmly through the soul of this girl of the cemetery: Marysia was clearly grateful that the fruit from her pear tree had been eaten and, as a token of thanks, had rewarded her with double the crop.

Magda, prudent as she was, did not share her joyful secret with her grandfather, but she went out again that evening and stealthily picked an apple from one of the sparsely fruited trees.

And it happened again, as she sensed in her tender heart that it would. Overnight, two hearty buds emerged from one of the tree's barren branches, and on the following day, two freshly ripened apples swayed to and fro under the caress of the rising sun.

And beneath that tree there rested a little boy, son of one of the townsmen. He slept his eternal sleep right alongside the children of the village, only his grave was more beautiful, having been presided over for many years by a large and striking angel standing atop his tombstone.

That little boy was evidently grateful that his apple tree was not disdained, for he also provided a twofold reward, and the face of the heavenly guardian whose wings spread wide over his grave

appeared somehow brighter and full of cheer . . . And so, day after
day, Magda picked a fruit from each of the various trees, and in
each case new fruit grew lavishly in place of the one she had eaten,
even though it was late autumn, an unusual time for new growth.

One clear night, when the moon's brilliance was spread
serenely over the sleeping world, Magda sat by the open window
of the cottage and gazed pensively into the silent orchard. Gregor
was already fast asleep in the adjoining room; in the corner by the
chimney a solitary cricket chirped, and the air hummed with the
silence of advancing night. A path of silvery sand extended from
the sky into the cemetery, penetrating the thicket of trees and
bushes. Green-tinged streams of moonlight trickled through the
foliage, illuminating the network of paths that crisscrossed this
way and that among the graves.

The soft, sensitive antennae of light glanced against the leaves
and grasses before bashfully retracting into limitless space. And
that which was touched shuddered with pleasure, undulating with
a silvery tremor . . .

The black tree trunks and bristling heads of bushes cast down
eerie nets of shadow, lying in wait for roaming prey. Swarms of
flies tiny as grains of sand hovered under the light, alternately
drifting upwards and plummeting downwards, meandering aim-
lessly, without purpose . . .

Under the trees on each grave, columns of white, translucent
mist rippled in the air: small children dressed in light tunics were
rising out of the ground. They emerged onto the surface of God's
green earth in their bright white shirts and steadied their bare feet
in the graveyard grass. Every one of them came out of his or her
underground sanctuary, with not a single child remaining behind
in its coffin. There was Marysia, the widow's daughter with eyes as
blue as cornflowers and hair as yellow as rye; there was that little
boy, the son of the townsfolk; and many, many others, rich and
poor, comely and ugly, urban and rural, but all dressed alike in
only a long shirt, and barefoot.

The cemetery was somehow brightened by these snow-white
surplices, which had a deeply solemn appearance. A great light
came from them, bathing the whole orchard in its brilliance.

Each of them stood under their tree, smiling a hazy but happy smile and, leaning a hand against its trunk, looked up between the glimmering, barren branches.

And under the power of that miraculous gaze, the autumnal buds began to sprout: firm shoots emerged and calyxes bloomed and spread their petals, until all of the pear, apple, and plum trees were bursting with fruit, just as in the happier times when the orchard was robust and plentiful.

Then the children took their hands off the trees and, stretching their arms out widely before them in a gesture of generous invitation, seemed to be saying collectively:

'Come, do not wait! Eat, and be healthy!'

And these wonderful things played out in hushed silence, by way of mute gestures, without so much as a murmur, as in a dream!

Tree limbs swaying in the wind cut through what seemed an airless space, while the children's windblown tunics fluttered in soft, soundless waves amid the sublunar radiance.

Magda rubbed her eyes, uncertain whether she was awake or dreaming, then reached out her hand and touched the window frame . . .

It was daylight, and sunshine streamed over her youthful, developed breasts, which peeked out inadvertently from beneath her shirt. She had been sitting at the window since the previous evening and now breathed in the sharpening crispness of the morning.

On the bushes and sedge-stalks, large translucent tears glistened – in the corners, near the walls, the last wisps of mist were melting away – overhead, the sky was a deep, vibrant blue . . .

There was no trace of the dead little boys and girls; everything had disappeared like the down of spurge-bushes scattered by the wind. But not entirely. For when she raised her dreamy eyes to the trees, she saw that they were bent under the weight of the fruit that had miraculously sprung forth overnight. The orchard was filled with an abundance it had not seen in years, laughing with its plentiful, enduring bounty.

Magda went to her sleeping grandfather, tugged at his robe to wake him up and then led him to the window. His face blushed with excitement and joy at the miracle. And then she told him of all that had happened, starting with the moment she dared to break his rule against eating the fruit.

The old man listened, looking from the trees to his granddaughter and back again, marveling at the profound love she carried in her heart. And he recognized in this a great lesson for himself and for everyone, for here was the first time that the ardent will of the dead had become clear to him. He obeyed it humbly, his soul filled with happiness and tranquility.

That day, they went out to call upon the people. Magda headed for the village, while Gregor went into town. They spent half the day enjoying themselves in this pursuit, and, when they returned home in the evening, Magda began to prepare supper while Gregor sat down by the stove. Having lit his pipe, he puffed on it quietly, watching his granddaughter bustle about the kitchen with a smile on his face. Finally, he asked:

'Did you invite any guests?'

'Indeed, I did. They all will come. There was a lot of joy and wonder. People didn't want to believe me, I barely managed to convince them.'

'Ain't that the truth. I wouldn't have believed it myself. What a story!'

He fell silent, sinking into his thoughts. Only after supper did he resume the conversation:

'It seems that they need us. Do you see? They want to establish some kind of bond with us from beyond the grave; they do not want to exist there uselessly. Therefore, they offer us what they can. We, in turn, offer up our prayers for them. Yes, yes ... how strangely it all connects, falls into place – a sacred communion with the dead ...'

He finished his pipe, shook out the ashes, and lay down heavily on the bed. But Magda sat up long into the night thinking about her grandfather's words, which had penetrated deeply into her soul. Eventually, she too succumbed to a sweet slumber which swept her off into oblivion ...

The next day, from the golden morning on, the cemetery orchard was bustling. Children in festive dress trickled in through the wide-open gates, either alone or clasping the hand of an elder; they flushed with curiosity, but also with a kind of reverent fear in their eyes.

From village and city alike, children of peasants and lords came for the communal feast, greeting each other as friends among the coolness of the autumnal trees, heavy with their yield. The orchard was abuzz with flecks of yellow, red, gray, green, or navy, and the clear, bright sound of children's voices.

When finally at about noon the space was packed with people, and from every corner pairs of dark or blue eyes glittered with impatience, Gregor gave the expected sign.

A few stout young fellows rushed to the trees, climbed up between the boughs and began to shake the harvest to the ground. Fruit rained down, tender and juicy, until it blanketed the ground. The whole cemetery teemed with vibrant motion: branches shuddering, treetops wobbling, children stepping up and bending down. A wonderful fragrance wafted through the orchard, and the exuberant trees stared proudly up at the sky; they were relieved to give their heavy burdens up to the winds, to play freely, joyfully – with a blissful maternal pride, they extended their arms over their generous offspring, over the heads of the children gathering it, over this beloved and life-giving land . . .

The sky above the peaks was already blushing with the redness of evening, the sun's slanting rays becoming entangled within the dense foliage, when the children began to file out the gate back onto the road, weighed down by the baskets, knotted cloths, and kerchiefs into which they had stuffed their ample haul. And for a long while afterwards, the sounds of shouting, singing, and hearty laughter continued to ring out from afar . . .

From that day on, the orchard yielded more and more bountiful harvests, never exhausting itself, and never tiring from the hard labor of creation . . .

Twice a year, the children of men came for the harvest: once at the beginning of summer, when the glowworms light up the bushes, and the linden trees give off their sweet fragrance, to pluck the sweet, juicy cherries, and the second time in autumn for the apples, pears, and plums. They came not as for everyday fruit-picking, but with pious joy, as befits a grand and cherished festival, in their Sunday dress, and with humility and reverence in their hearts.

And they called this festival 'The Orchards', and the old cemetery 'The Orchard of the Dead.' And the cemetery was bright and cheerful, basking in heavenly bliss, like a sacred grove of the gods, rich in crops, vibrant with birds chirping and bees buzzing, beloved by the people. For it was quiet and bountiful, and gave forth fruit in abundance, because of the grace of the dead who lay within it.

Ksenia

A Bachelor's Adventure

Commissioner Przetocki was having a marvelous day. He felt
healthy and fresh, his appetite was splendid, and his funds
were ample. He had received his expected raise, rounding off his
monthly income quite nicely. The Bureau Chief had called him
in personally this morning for a private chat to inform him of his
likely promotion in the near future, at the same time dropping a
few words, as if unintentionally, about his middle daughter, blue-
eyed Natalia, charming and well-dowried, an ideal match for the
young commissioner. In a word, it was smooth sailing all the way
– a good career, a fine marriage prospect; he had all of his relation-
ships and alliances 'in the bag', so to speak. All was well with the
world . . .

Smiling blissfully beneath his mustache, Przetocki strolled over
the soft, green carpet of grass covering the suburban pasture. Adrift
on the sea of his thoughts, he had long passed the tollgate and begun
a solitary ramble across the vast grassland stretching from just outside the village to the edge of the forest on the distant horizon.

It was a beautiful August day. Warmed by the afternoon sun,
the grateful earth returned the sky's favors by offering up aromas
of mint and centaury, along with intermingled odors of thistle, St.
John's wort, and wild roses.

It was five in the afternoon, that extraordinary hour of the
summer season when the sun's heat has relented and a sweet golden
warmth spreads over the world – an hour of solace after the swelter
of the early afternoon; a soothing, autumn-like time of leisure just
before sunset. The landscape, saturated by the day-long sowing of
the sun's rays, took on a calm, settled appearance: the breathless

rush of heat-swollen clouds across the vast blue sky had ceased, the intensity of their blinding-white faces diminished, and they had settled into an even shoal far off to the north. Only a few playful 'little lambs' scattered in the middle of the sky traced pinkish furrows across the turquoise firmament while, beyond the forest, where the sun was completing its triumphant arc, the snowy peak of a lone cloud protruded from below the treeline . . .

The silence of the pasture was broken by the jangling of bells around the necks of grazing cows, or the distant calls of shepherds from beyond the rolling hills. Occasionally a frog croaked in a puddle, contemplating its marshy lot, or an unbridled horse wallowed in the shrubbery . . .

Przetocki cast cheerful, friendly glances at his surroundings, breathing in the fresh scents of grass and herbs as he walked toward the forest. He reached a cluster of blackthorns on a small hill and, feeling a bit weary, took off his hat and plunged into the shade of the bushes. He lay on his back, resting his head on his arms, and gazed up at the sky.

A light breeze from the forest cooled his face and caused the bushes to rustle softly, lulling Przetocki into drowsiness. He might have fallen asleep, were it not for the sustained sound of a voice, full of sadness and strange longing, that had suddenly rung out just beside the blackthorn thicket. It was a woman singing.

Her voice was strong and fresh, though simple and untrained, clearly from a young breast. The song was some wistful ballad, a melody of the boundless steppes, wild and tender at the same time.

Carefully he pushed aside some branches to get a look at the singer. In a hollow just a few feet away sat a young country girl with a curiously noble profile. Her black satin eyes were fixed somewhere at the edge of the horizon as she sang her sorrowful song. The melody reached its peak as the tones rose to an intense pitch and the final, despairing chord rang out. She put all her soul into it. Her breast, heaving high, expelled a gale of sounds imbued with boundless pain, profoundly insatiable longing. The wandering plight of this bereft soul wound its way through the ravines, carrying with it a passionate desire for happiness, and a creeping flame of unslaked fervor . . .

Then she broke off, frightened by the rustling caused by his careless movements. Przetocki came out of his hiding spot and met her fearful, bleary-eyed gaze. She was beautiful, very much so. Delicate features, a pale, almost transparent complexion, black hair with a tarry sheen blowing freely in the wind, her whole figure as lithe as a reed, she exuded an indescribable charm. She was dressed very shabbily; her skirt, faded by sun and rain, was so tattered that it failed to properly cover her body; her small, bare feet were caked in mud and scratched in several places from thistles and thorn bushes. He liked her very much, taking her in with a predatory, lustful gaze:

'Good evening, miss.'

She didn't respond right away. Her doleful eyes gradually lost their expression of terror and began to examine him carefully.

'Franek!'

She closed her eyes in a kind of rapture, and a moment later she was embracing him with the full weight of her body, repeating softly with unspeakable delight:

'Franek!'

Przetocki was entranced. He pulled her close to him and stifled the soft, sweet whispers coming out of her mouth with his own lips.

'Let's go,' he said in a firm, confident voice.

'Let's go,' she repeated softly, submissively.

And they went together into the dark forest nearby. On the way, she frequently leaned in toward him, kissing his hands, nuzzling him like a dog.

'Franek! Franek! My darling . . .'

The Commissioner didn't analyze, he didn't think; he only desired, longed to be satiated, intoxicated. He was overcome by a dizzying, hot-blooded euphoria, aroused by the fire of her yearning eyes. When he wondered for a fleeting instant why she kept calling him Franek, he dismissed the thought by reasoning that it must simply be a name she liked, and which she'd applied to him as a term of endearment. Then he continued to let himself be carried away on the wave of passion enveloping them both . . .

Entering the forest, they turned down a side path – in their haste they nearly ran through a section lined with ferns and plunged into a shadowy recess. Przetocki wanted to go on to some place deeper in the woods, when suddenly, out of breath, she dropped onto the grass.

He leaned over her, embraced her with trembling arms, and their desire reached a crescendo. She yielded with wild abandon, pleasure bordering on madness; her small coral lips clenched in spasmodic, painful contractions, her face in its frenzy of lust alternated between a hot-blooded glow and a deathly pallor. There were moments when her body, stretched like a bowstring, stiffened so tautly in its love-throes that she looked like a corpse. But a second later the string would snap and slacken, closing around him in a red-hot band.

Przetocki went wild. This strange girl's boundless love captivated him. Her glazed-over eyes exuded a sweet allure which ignited a fire within him. He was intoxicated by the richness of her lust, the insatiability of her desire. She was inexhaustible in kisses, devilishly imaginative in her caresses. Overcome and unrestrained, he responded with a force that was brutal, primal, ruthless, and he could feel that she was grateful for it! . . . At last, he was exhausted. He leaned his back against a tree and began mindlessly running his eyes over the woman's splayed-out body. He was roused from his torpor by the sound of gentle sobbing: she was crying. Instinctively, he took her hand in his. She responded with a spasmodic clench:

'Franek! Oh, Franek! You dragon! Come on, let's go again.'

'I can't. I have to get home, it's already late.' He looked at his watch. 'Seven o'clock. It'll be dark soon.'

With some effort, he raised himself from the base of the tree, stretched lazily, and yawned.

'Well then, let's get going.'

Silently she sat up, hugging him around the legs.

'All right then, it's all right.' He stroked her hair tenderly. 'We really should get back now.' They headed out together, and upon emerging from the woods, Przetocki attempted to take his leave.

'We'll have to part ways here. Someone might see us together. Be well!'

'Franek!' she whispered pleadingly. 'Franek!'

'Well, what's wrong?'

'Franek, I'll go back to town with you.'

'To town? What for?'

'I can serve you. Franek, bring me with you!'

'That's impossible. I have a wife,' he snapped, lying.

'I don't care. I'll serve you both, loyal as a dog. Don't leave me here, at God's mercy! Franek, I can't live without you!'

'Nonsense!' he retorted. 'We have to part here.'

She didn't answer, her bare feet mincing along in hurried steps to keep pace with him.

Przetocki was angry. He resented the girl's intrusion. A flash of anxiety shone in his sharp, gray eyes.

They reached a back road which ran through a suburban hamlet and wound in the distance towards the town. He doubled his pace, thinking that this would discourage her, but he was wrong; unable to keep up, she periodically broke into a run. At that point, he resorted to threats. These had no effect; the girl continued to accompany him with a bizarre obstinacy. So he fell silent and with furrowed brow continued down the dusty road. An old woman emerged from a cottage with some watering cans, headed for a well. Noticing them, she stopped and said in greeting:

'God be with you!'

'And with you!' he answered, not slowing his pace.

'What are you doing hanging around with that girl? For shame! God help you!'

'Ha, well, ma'am,' he responded, stopping. 'I can't seem to get rid of her. She's been following me like a shadow.'

'Sir, leave her alone. She's that crazy Ksenia – a lunatic.'

'Lunatic?!' Przetocki blanched, shuddering.

'Oh yes, lunatic indeed. Last year she was courted by that Franek Luśwa, the blacksmith's apprentice. He had his fun with her for a few weeks, then vanished like a stone in water. She's been missing him terribly, and the good Lord's got her mind all mixed up. A godly scourge, it is. She wanders all around the countryside looking for that bastard. He'll get his just deserts, God willing!'

Przetocki couldn't stand another word.

'God bless you, ma'am!' he shouted as he walked off, turning down a side path. Ksenia continued to follow him tirelessly. He turned and, noticing that the old woman was no longer visible on the main road, took off running back down it. A wild fear propelled his legs and bore his feet along:

'Ksenia, crazy! Crazy!'

Behind him he heard the patter of her bare feet over the loose dirt, her breathless panting:

'Franek, don't run away!'

He hastened on without pausing. An approaching carriage loomed in the distance, headed for town. A glimmer of hope flashed in his tired brain.

As it passed, he yelled at the driver, who stopped. With his last remnants of strength he rushed forward, reached the vehicle and hopped in.

'To town! Full speed!'

The whip cracked, the horses neighed, and the carriage began rolling.

The Commissioner turned to look back. Ksenia was still running down the road in a rush of despair, a hopeless effort. Suddenly she stumbled and fell, disappearing amid a cloud of dust, ash-gray dirt from the road infused with copper beams of sunlight . . .

The horses tore off in a gallop, passed the bend, and wound their way among the lanes on the periphery of town. In a quarter of an hour, Przetocki arrived back home. He took off his sweaty, dust-covered clothes, changed his undergarments, and washed himself, perpetually shivering as though with fever. Then he went over to the window and, leaning his hands heavily on the desk, hung his head. The old country woman's words buzzed irksomely in his ears like wasps, and fear choked him.

'What a story! A fine mess I'm in!'

He remembered one particular way in which Ksenia had caressed him, and his entire frame trembled:

'She could have really hurt me! Crazy Ksenia, that madwoman!'

She had ruined his entire evening. He was supposed to attend a soiree at his superior's house at ten o'clock! He couldn't go now. He was too wound up.

'Curse the whole wretched affair!' he exclaimed fervidly.

And the windows were aflame with the glow of the day's dying sun. Bloody spurts of light poured in through the panes and puddled morosely on the floor. Amid their purplish streams a pair of hands writhed painfully, fingers contorted in bottomless grief; from their depths deranged eyes surveyed the empty distance, the roving plight of the abandoned and forlorn . . .

On the Trail

I woke up with my head heavy as lead, feeling brutally exhausted. I looked at the clock: twelve noon. I had slept unusually late today.

The house was suffused with the quiet of the sweltering noon, the drowsy torpor of the July heat. I was alone. Old Jan had gone off, as usual, to drop in on one of the neighbors for an after-lunch pipe, leaving me at the mercy of Providence.

With immense difficulty I put my hands under my head, staring at the ceiling. Some kind of monstrous exhaustion held down my hands and feet like a set of gigantic weights, preventing me from getting up out of bed.

I thought back to the previous day, but recalled nothing that could have caused this truly extraordinary lassitude of the limbs. I had passed a quiet day painting landscapes; in the evening, I took a short moonlit stroll around the city, and then went to sleep around ten o'clock. That was all.

Nothing notable there. Something else was behind this. Was I ill, perhaps? But how could that be?

My gaze detached from the mosaic on the ceiling and automatically fell upon the steel screen erected in the middle of the room. It was my hypnoscope. In my free time I devote myself to the study of the fascinating field of hypnosis and have already achieved quite promising results, particularly with regard to self-induced sleep. All it takes is for me to direct a few focused glances at the screen to induce instantaneous sleep, from which I can then awaken at a predetermined hour.

Of late, however, I've stopped the practice, having noticed that it has a disruptive effect on my body, causing me to feel a bit strange and out of sorts upon waking.

Nevertheless, apparently something had tempted me yesterday to resume experimenting after an extended break. At least, that's what the positioning of the screen in the center of the room indicated, as I usually keep it pushed up against the wall.

What perturbed me, however, was that I had no memory of whether I had actually stared at the hypnoscope last night. In any case, it must have been after I returned from my walk, around ten o'clock at night. And yet, the last thing I recall doing was taking off my overcoat and hanging it on the rack.

What happened after that, I do not remember. I presume the urge for self-hypnosis came to me from somewhere, and I did not fail to satisfy it.

So, that explained my situation, and somewhat accounted for my weariness. The only question was what I had actually been dreaming about, and what exactly had happened to me during that time. Again I was troubled by the peculiar amnesia that always afflicted my brain upon waking: I could never remember anything.

And my undertakings while in this hypnotic state must have been very involved at times. I became convinced of this by first-hand observation in a strange, almost accidental way.

One day, upon waking in the morning, I was astonished to find the torso of some old statue on the scaffolding by my easels. The stone was weathered and scratched in places, yet I could still see the traces of a master's hand in its fabulously carved lines. At first, I could not figure out how this piece of stone had ended up in my studio. I thought that perhaps some acquaintance had wanted to play a prank on me, or that Jan had gotten the urge to amuse me with this piece of art. But all of my inquiries led nowhere; everyone shrugged their shoulders and looked at me as if I were a madman.

So I subjected this particular acquisition to careful inspection and, after some time, concluded that I had seen this fragment – with its head tragically missing – somewhere before. A few years earlier, while passing by an old park in a remote district of the city, I had noticed a heavily weathered statue with no arms, barely attached to the partially crumbled pedestal that served as its base. The piece nonetheless caught my eye and made an impression. For some time I even entertained the idea of rendering the piece in a painting. Then I completely forgot about it.

It probably happened that, at the moment of falling asleep, in that last instant marking the transition from waking to sleep, an image of the statue had flashed through my mind, perhaps combined with a desire to acquire it. This last thought, which came into being just upon the threshold of consciousness, I must have dragged behind me like a trawling net into the murky abyss of sleep, where autosuggestion transformed into an irresistible command. I had then gone out and brought the object back with me.

I was able to verify the statue's identity during one of my walks, which I deliberately took shortly afterwards in the direction of the aforementioned park. Here I found everything as it had been years before; but in the place where the disfigured torso had once stood, there remained nothing but a bare pedestal; only the ferns, having flourished high above the banks of a nearby stream, enveloped it in their greenery, as if shamefully covering its white nakedness.

To this day, I still cannot understand how I managed to move the heavy stone trunk from the park to my workshop; it truly would have required immense strength. There must have been some mad, uncompromising inner compulsion at work, some categorical imperative permitting of no reflection or hesitation; a hundredfold multiplication of strength, all sinews straining in a frenzied effort to satisfy, to fulfill, an injunction that had burned itself into the recesses of my soul; a frenetic, uncanny power that heaves up and plunges headlong through overgrown paths and uprooted trees, breaking, smashing, pulverizing everything that stands in its way, finally reaching its goal breathless and dripping with blood, but triumphant . . .

What disturbed me most about this bizarre occurrence, however, was the apparent intensification of this last, perhaps even rather fleeting hypnagogic thought to the status of an internal command. Everything depended on this last thought, which had strayed almost to the very threshold of sleep . . .

I rose sluggishly from my bed and began to dress.

A moment later, I noticed to my surprise that I had put on formal attire instead of my usual, everyday clothes. Had Jan deliberately prepared them for me today? I did not recall having given him any special instructions to this effect, nor had I called upon anyone yesterday. Perhaps, then, he thought that my everyday clothes had already become too threadbare, and that it was not appropriate for me to present myself in them, even on an average workday. In general, he was quite uncompromising in his dealings with me. A good-natured, simple soul!

I felt so beat up that I didn't feel like changing into anything else, so I put on my freshly tailored, raven-black frock coat.

I found myself vaguely ill at ease; some indefinable feeling of aversion or disgust had been troubling me since the moment I woke up; my mouth felt coated with a repulsively bitter taste.

I walked around the room a few times to shake off these unpleasant sensations and regain my equilibrium. At one point I passed the mirror and, having glanced at it inadvertently, was horrified at what I beheld: I was pale as a corpse; my eyes were shining with an overstimulated, phosphorescent glow, and my hands were making peculiar movements. I watched them carefully, extending them on a line parallel to my hips, as my fingers twitched nervously so that it appeared as though I were dropping something. I was only able to observe this briefly because, having noticed it, I took control of myself almost violently and shoved my hands into my pockets. Some kind of nervous delirium? . . .

From the hallway came the characteristic grunting and smacking of lips on a pipe: Jan was coming back from his chat. After a moment he came in, evidently not very happy with me.

'So, you've finally pulled yourself together! Good Lord – sleeping till noon! I couldn't wake you up. There was some young gentleman here, tall fellow, skinny as a corpse. Said something about paintings. I told him the master was sleeping, to come back later. He wouldn't let up. So I started to jostle you a bit, to no avail. A real iron slumber God sent you last night. Stone-cold sleep!'

'Right you are, Jan. I was dead asleep. But why on earth did you change out my clothes? I didn't request that yesterday.'

The old man looked at me bewildered, apparently only now noticing that I was clad in formal attire.

'I, change them out? I dare say it must have been you who . . .'

Here he made a clear sign on his forehead. 'I only cleaned what I found on the chair this morning. These must have been new – yes, they are new.'

He paused, searching his memory.

'Wait a minute; it's coming to me ... Wait ... Oh, yes ... Yes, that's right. Yesterday evening, to the best of my recollection, you wore that casual jacket, the velvet one. My word! It must have been you yourself who put that one away before going to bed, then laid out these for today and forgot about it!'

He spoke calmly as usual, with his cordial, benevolently nagging tone. But at times his eyes rested on me with a certain bemusement, as though curious about something.

'All right, all right. Yes – I must have changed out the clothes myself, but now I can't remember why. I'll have my breakfast, please. Are today's papers here?'

'Yes, they are. The boy has just brought them. He also slipped a most extraordinary supplement, a telegram or something of the sort, into my hand. I took it because I thought you might be interested. I'll bring everything right away.'

Within a few minutes, a steaming cup of coffee had been set on the table with the newspapers spread out invitingly around it.

I drank the coffee and, lighting a cigarette, began to read the papers. I happened upon the 'extraordinary' supplement, issued remarkably early in the day, even before the morning edition. The heading declared, in bold print, a sensational incident:

TRAGIC DEATH OF COUNTESS V. S.

As a rule, I contemptuously avoid any articles pertaining to crime; I dislike any bloody business redolent of morgues or hospitals. As such, I was about to set this curious incident aside when my fleeting glance at the rows of black letters landed upon a single word. It was the name of a certain suburban locality which was associated in my mind with several distant, yet rather firmly imprinted memories.

I picked up the disagreeable notice and read the following rather succinct announcement:

Last night, a strange and tragic incident occurred at Wygnanka. This morning, in one of the chambers of the 'Red Castle', the hereditary property of the counts of S., the body of the twenty-year-old Countess Valeria was found. She died as a result of a dagger thrust directly into her heart. No other injuries were found on the body. The case remains shrouded in mystery. We will provide more details in the morning edition.

The name that drew my attention was the above-mentioned 'Wygnanka', a kind of hamlet or suburban grange less than a mile outside the city. Although I had been in this area only once in my life, it had left such a strong impression that the connection of its name with a sensational incident compelled me to take a closer look at the matter.

The 'Red Castle' was associated in my mind with the memory of a beautiful woman I had once seen years ago. Could she have been the victim of the previous night's tragedy?

I picked up the morning edition hoping to find more specific information. This is what I read:

A MYSTERIOUS CRIME!

The terrible incident that occurred at the 'Red Castle' late Wednesday night bears the stamp of something mysterious. Following a detailed investigation, the possibility of suicide was ruled out; Miss Valeria S. fell victim to some vindictive, murderous hand. This is borne out by the spine-chilling facts we are about to relate.

When Lady Maria S. returned to the castle this morning at about 8 a.m. after a day's absence, she found a group of servants at the entrance gate in a state of anxious confusion; their collective faces met Lady S.'s eyes with a look of unspoken terror. Sensing that something was not right, Lady S. asked after her beloved daughter Valeria, whom she had left at home, contrary to habit. Then the old nursemaid Nastusia spoke up on behalf of the others, declaring with a tremor in her voice that the girl had either overslept or, God forbid, fainted, as she had not emerged from her room, despite having announced the night before that she would be waking up early to greet her mother. No one had dared to wake her, and in any case, the girl had locked the door from the inside, and there was no other means of entry into the room.

Worried, Lady S. immediately rushed upstairs and started to violently rattle the handle of her daughter's bedroom door. When after several such attempts there was no answer from within, she bade everyone be silent and put her ear to the key-hole to listen for the sleeping girl's breathing. But inside there was a deafening silence. Terrified, she then ordered the bolted doors to be forced open at once. Upon entering the room, Lady S. immediately looked toward her daughter's bed. The unfortunate woman was thunderstruck by what she saw.

Under a carpet of white lilies, Valeria lay on her back with her hands folded as if in prayer. The handle of a dagger protruded from her breast, in the area of her heart; clotted bloodstains peered out from under the flowers, on the quilt, the upper hem of her shirt, and the white woolen rug. The poor girl looked asleep: eyes closed, face tranquil, without a trace of pain, she simply appeared to be in a state of deep rest. But the steel-pierced heart did not beat; a corpse lay in that bed.

Alerted by a telephone call from the mother, who was almost out of her mind with grief, the police department sent a commissioner and team of investigators to the crime scene. According to the medical examiner, Miss Valeria died from a remarkably precise dagger strike nearly six inches deep into her right ventricle. It was a forceful thrust – the dagger was plunged in up to the hilt. Most likely, death occurred instantaneously, without the victim waking up. This is evidenced by her closed eyes and serene facial expression.

The investigators concluded that the attack was carried out after midnight, between two and three o'clock in the morning.

The police in turn began their search for the assailant, running into difficulties right from the outset. First of all was the question of motive. Robbery, or any other pecuniary motive, was definitively ruled out; nothing was found to have been disturbed either in the bedroom or the whole castle. So it must have been a crime of vengeance or jealousy. Here the question arose: was the perpetrator a man or a woman? A question to which no one has yet been able to give a definite answer. The deceased was a woman of extraordinary beauty; she must undoubtedly have had many female enemies and regularly inspired rivalries among men.

At first it was thought that the lilies covering the corpse would point in some direction: an odd detail, laden with gloomy, sepulchral poetry. But this appears to have been a dead end; most regarded it merely as a clever device to put the investigators on a false trail. Perhaps the future will bring greater clarity to this. Overall, we must say that this horrifying tragedy at the 'Red Castle' is marked by a number of eerie and enigmatic features.

Above all, it is not known how the assailant was able to gain entry to Miss Valeria's bedroom. As her mother testified during the investigation, she found the bedroom bolted from the inside in the morning. Upon leaving the day before, she had ordered her daughter to lock her door overnight so as to isolate herself from the servants, who slept downstairs. Adjacent to her bedroom is a long row of rooms that have stood empty since the death of the master of the house. These are apparently occupied by relatives during family reunions. But there have been no visitors within the last few days; there was only Miss Valeria's maid, Małgorzata, who slept in the room adjoining the lady's bedroom and claims to have heard nothing suspicious. The door is the only entrance to the room, and the windows were found locked in the morning just as they had been in the evening. Even if we assume that the assailant managed to sneak into the castle by some strange means, perhaps in collusion with one of the servants, we are faced with the insoluble mystery of how he managed to get into the bedroom through the bolted door or the closed windows without making noise and waking the victim.

Let us hope nevertheless that our skilled agents will soon lead the investigation down the right track and shed brighter light upon this dark affair. We will offer a detailed synopsis of the investigation in our evening edition.

Having skimmed through this write-up of the case, I turned the page to look upon the image of the murdered woman, which had been printed a bit further on.

A mere glance at the victim's face was all it took to confirm my
suspicions as to her identity: I knew this Miss Valeria; she was the
same woman I had glimpsed for a brief moment two years earlier,
never to see again in life. And yet, the strong impression I felt then
had left an indelible trace.

This was in the form of a painting inspired by the sight of this
woman of ideal beauty, executed soon after during an hours-long
bout of intense creative work. This creation was an act of liberation for me: after finishing it, I was able to breathe easy and turn
to more cheerful topics. My memory of Valeria began to recede
behind a thicker and thicker veil, so that the whole affair finally
seemed naught but a fleeting vision. Today, under the influence
of her terrible death, the memories came back to life, stirring up
echoes that had long died away.

I raised the blinds and, sitting down by the window, began to
study as closely as possible the image captured at the scene of the
crime. The engraving was done perfectly. Although it had been
two years since I last saw the unfortunate woman, her features,
rendered with remarkable fidelity, left no shadow of doubt. It
was the same face, resembling in its subtlety the ascetic visages of
holy virgins, like ovals cut from wax of immaculate whiteness, the
same cool, marble forehead anointed with a balm of undisturbed
serenity. Strangely in tune with this expression were the head-
dress and the satin cushion beneath it which, owing to a peculiar
arrangement of folds and creases, gave the appearance of a broad,
white cornette surrounding her. The hands crossed tranquilly over
her breast completed this image of pristine, dignified death. She
looked like a saint of a holy order rejoicing in her liberation from
this sinful earth, smiling before the pleasures of heaven.

Slowly, amid a rush of suppositions, speculations and conjectures, a strong, insatiable desire to visit the scene of the crime
forced its way into my thoughts. A mad curiosity urged me toward
the gloomy setting of that nocturnal deed and compelled me to
investigate the situation.

I took off my light cloth shoes and reached under the bed for
my boots. Imagine my surprise when, instead of my usual walking
boots, I found the shiny new dress shoes I had purchased a few days

earlier. Furious, I flung them away and yanked open one of my
dresser drawers, hoping to find my everyday shoes there. But the
search was fruitless; I could not find them anywhere. So I gave up,
and not wanting to waste any more time on the search, put on the
accursed shiny ones and left the house by the front door, locking
it behind me.

Half an hour later I was on the road that wound like a long,
white ribbon towards Wygnanka.

It was around three o'clock. The picturesqueness of the
landscape, heightened by the play of the sun's rays, gave me an
impression that was at odds with what I should have expected; I
greeted everything I saw with unpleasant recognition, a sense of
disagreeable familiarity. At the same time I was bothered by a feeling that something was not right with the lighting: it felt intensely
exaggerated and therefore somehow different, inappropriate.
In my imagination, I began to apply alternate exposures to the
scene, trying to restore the 'proper' mood and spirit to things. And
thereby, so gradually as to be almost imperceptible, the reddish-
yellow streaks the sun had cast over the plowed fields turned a pale
blue, and finally radiated the silver-green glow of the moon. The
world darkened for a moment, turned a deep and gloomy blue,
before sparkling again with the brilliance of a moonlit night.

At some point, my gait seemed to change; it ceased to be a natural movement driven by my own conscious will and took on the
character of something wooden: I found myself walking stiffly,
like an automaton. With my arms outstretched before me, I proceeded forward, pointing my hands toward the destination . . .

On my left stretched fields of wheat steeped in mist, the ears
rustling furtively as they swished in the wind . . .

On my right extended an old white wall, first of a cemetery,
then of a park or a garden, creating one interminably long line.
Viburnum branches, having pushed their way through the decaying framework, wavered gently in the wind, confiding to the night
the sorrow of their garden of death. Delicate willow sprigs swaying in the summer breeze wept down the wall as though lamenting
humanity's doleful plight. A shrunken shadow moved along the
walls, climbed to the top and then lengthened until it disappeared

in the orchard. Phantom forms flickered menacingly on the lime-washed wall. They recognized me from afar and made signs beckoning me towards them. Their monstrous jaws snapped open and shut, their shaggy hands twisted into claws like a sparrowhawk's, then they were running forward again, inviting me to follow them – evil, giggling, elusive . . .

Suddenly, the ground beneath my feet rattled and rumbled: I was walking over a bridge. This lonely clattering amidst the bottomless silence of the world was so terrible that I hunched over, seized by a wild trepidation; I plugged my ears and started to run so as not to hear it anymore. I could not stand this rumbling; it reminded me of something horrible and felt all too familiar, though not defined by any particular place or time.

I reached the other end of the bridge and plunged into an alley of poplars.

Their limber tops waved to and fro majestically in the wind, whispering to one another. Unsteady on my feet, I made my way out of the alley and stopped just as I emerged. The night had vanished, the spectral moonlight had faded, the rapacious shadows had receded: I was by the castle, near a pond, on a warm, sunny afternoon.

I rubbed my eyes, unsure whether I was dreaming, and set off along the walls. The castle looked somewhat more accessible from this direction; otherwise, it was protected on all sides by steep, sloping walls. It was connected to the road by a drawbridge, which during the night would be retracted to the bastions. It was only from here, on the south side, that a break in the wall gave way to an exterior wall supporting one side of the fortress.

So from this spot it would have been possible for the murderer to reach as far as halfway up the castle. But there was still a long way to go up to the first window, and the wall was completely smooth, with no trace of any indentations.

I hung my head helplessly, struggling against a thousand conjectures. There was nothing else to do but to suppose that the criminal had acted while in a state of extraordinarily enhanced ability, under the pressure of a furiously concentrated nervous force which could enable him to traverse surfaces smooth as glass, balance over the precipice, and unfasten the window bolts from outside, moving nimbly, silently, irresistibly, fiercely . . . I could not solve the riddle.

Discouraged, especially after noticing a few individuals wandering around nearby who had been following my movements with curiosity for some time, I turned back to the road and soon was passing again between the rows of poplars.

Tranquil and stolid, the sun peeked through the rows of trees as they disappeared into the distance, marking the seconds by the casting of shadows. Somewhere, a woodpecker hammered away at a hollow, a cuckoo's call portended good luck. It was five o'clock, and the afternoon was golden and warm.

'Where did that moonlit nightmare come from?' I thought feverishly.

I thought it most likely that I had entered into the state of the criminal's soul as he embarked upon his deed by night, beneath the moon, and experienced his torment. The vividness and intensity of the situation only testified to my own sensitivity. The course of the murderer's experiences that I had apparently reenacted was drawn directly from my analysis of the facts reported in the newspaper. Everything seemed to fit together. And yet, deep down, I was haunted by some half-conscious thoughts – keen, logical, obstinate – that put the lie to everything.

But I pretended that everything was in order, and enjoyed the peace of an untroubled surface. Indeed, I'd had enough of all this. The tragedy of Wygnanka had drawn me too personally into its vortices, so that I was afraid I would be absorbed by it. Why, after all, should I give a damn about the whole affair? What did it have to do with me? I had to distance myself from it.

But my thoughts continued to run in circles, moving only obliquely toward the sore point. An unbearable feeling of unease had thrust images cold as steel into my soul and begun to steadily tighten its net around me when an external detail suddenly diverted my attention to something else and, to my profound joy, did not allow me to complete the association.

When I came to within a few steps of that dreadful bridge, I felt that I would not be able to cross it.

The fear of hearing that rumbling, which resonated dully in the recesses of my brain, caused me to jerk back violently. There was no other way but to go beneath it.

Without a second thought, I left the road and started to descend into a ditch, which was thankfully completely dry. As I made my way down the lushly overgrown embankment, I noticed that someone had preceded me in this. The turf was torn up in places, and it clearly bore the marks of footsteps from someone sliding down the slope.

Since the ditch was dry, the footprints broke off just below the slope. However, I found that the tracks resumed closer to the bridge under which the river threaded before it disappeared further along among the boundless wastelands.

So someone else had broken off from the road just before the bridge. Strange! Perhaps for the same reasons?

The alluring possibility induced me to continue following the trail, so having jumped over the narrow strip of water, I did not return to the road, but struck off in the direction the tracks led. Looking at them more closely, I decided that they had been made by a man's shoe, and were a little wider than my shiny new leather ones.

At first they followed the side of the ditch parallel to the road, but then the trail veered abruptly toward the fields and wastes, clearly imprinted within the moist, clayey soil.

Following a pleasant night it had obviously rained in the morning, soaking the ground; the road had dried out quickly, while the loamy earth below had retained its latent moisture.

Although the way was extremely arduous, the unknown traveler did not return to the road, but pushed his way through boggy, barren fields without trails, borders, or signposts, as if robotically continuing in his chosen direction.

I would not have followed his example, had it not been for curiosity as to where it would lead me.

I soon began to wonder about his inconsistent course; it strayed to the right, to the left, jumped abruptly from one direction to another, tracing bizarre zigzags. Finally, it formed a violent arc which, having made a wide circle around the field, returned to its starting point.

I had an interesting puzzle in front of me. Either this was a trail made by some maniac, or by a man lost in deep thought about something.

Maybe the stubborn thought, having traversed a circular course, came back to stand again at the gate of his tormented brain: maybe the wanderer was fatally possessed by some idea which would not let him break free of the vicious circle, despite his efforts?

I stood at the center of this mysterious circle and looked ahead.

Slowly, the coiled trail slackened and crept staggeringly forward. The possessed man had broken the magic circle at last and, freeing himself with difficulty, had begun moving according to his own will. Somehow the sinuous course began to even out, the steps became more sure and, with remarkable swiftness, continued in the direction of the town.

I could not keep pace with his inhuman leaps, with a space of several meters between each one; this man was evidently fleeing from something. But I did not let him out of my sight, and followed right behind him.

It was rough going, and it became hard even to lift my feet. The loamy and only partially dried earth clung to my shoes, which soon became covered with reddish clay.

I was sad.

Thoughts drifted through my tormented mind like clouds of fog whipped into motion by violent winds; lights upraised by unknown hands flickered and went out.

I could already hear the bustle of the city in the distance, and the prolonged wailing of factory sirens as they slowly died away. I picked up another sound as well, plaintive and sustained ... I recognized it. It was the trumpeter playing a bugle call in honor of the Virgin Mary from the parish tower. A solemn, venerable melody ...

I started to examine my surroundings more carefully. The trail, it seemed, now led back toward the road that I had left some time ago. As far as I could discern from my position, I had already passed the line of breweries on the outskirts of the town, which I was now approaching from the wastelands on the other side.

I walked with bated breath, expecting that at any moment the

trail would veer off away from the field and wind up at some residence.

Suddenly my heart began to pound.

My surroundings now felt very familiar; I recognized the back
lots of houses overlooking the gardens and orchards.

I quickened my step with my eyes fixed on the strange trail, suppressing the uproar of thoughts forcing their way into my mind . . .

Suddenly I came upon some kind of barrier. I looked up and
found myself at the gate of my own garden. I flung it open and
stepped inside. The trail continued without interruption until it
reached the door of my own house.

I tugged at the door. It was locked.

Some atoms, until now dispersed, scattered like iron filings,
became polarized with accursed swiftness, carried away by currents coming from afar. I could feel the inexorable approach of the
wave that would bring order to the chaos.

I stood helplessly at the threshold for some time, not taking my
eyes off the footprints; they all led to the house, and the house was
locked.

Then I glanced to the left of the entrance and noticed new lines
of tracks; one began a bit farther from the threshold and led into
the garden, while the other apparently returned from there, crossing the first one and reaching the entrance again, only entirely
from a sidelong direction, so that at first I did not notice it.

I followed the first trail into the garden, where it soon turned
the corner of the house and went in among the flower beds.

Suddenly I let out a cry; the trail had ended at my favorite bed
of white lilies. But my bright flowers were gone – some terrible
hand had torn them all up, leaving only a mass of broken stems
behind.

'It was him!'

I rushed back to the house, desperate to get inside. I did not
bother looking for a key, but with a frantic burst of strength forced
the door open, breaking it off the hinges, and stumbled in.

I began once again to look for something. I went through the
closet, all the drawers in the table and desk, and any hiding place I
could find; then I went into Jan's room and searched through heaps

of his personal odds and ends, books, undergarments. I found nothing.

By chance, my eyes fell on the blackened door of the stove.

'Maybe there?'

I almost tore off the metal door as I greedily thrust my hands into its depths.

At last, deep, deep inside, I encountered something solid. I yanked at it, tore it out … It was a small bundle: my boots, encrusted up to the ankles with red clay, and my everyday clothes with the velvet jacket.

I unrolled the soft, crumpled …

'Yes, it was me!'

It was spattered with Valeria's blood.

Mud Hut in a Clear Field

Kuźma Żębroń, otherwise known as Red, had been walking for over a dozen hours already without rest. He'd wandered through forests in the morning, descended into ravines in the afternoon, and finally emerged again into the fields toward evening, proceeding continually onward. It seemed as if he would never tire of this walking. He had already traveled tens of miles, thousands of kilometers away from the place of his deeds, and still he forged ahead as if possessed.

All around him, the November night was as black and evil as his own soul. It had come upon him by surprise as he walked through a field of wild grasses and weeds. It was so dark he couldn't see his own hands, and raining buckets to boot.

Red had long since struck off from the dirt path and begun walking blindly in the dark. His feet, in clodhoppers heavy with the water that kept sloshing in over their tops, by turns got stuck in the clayey ground, slid down inclines, and sank to the ankles in the muddy pits left by toppled trees.

Soaked to the gills, hungry, freezing cold, and dog-tired, Żębroń trudged through the dreary autumn night with every ounce of strength he had left. But he did not lose his sense of fancy. What did he care about the pouring rain and the desolate night? He wasn't made of sugar; he wouldn't dissolve. These things didn't trouble him. He'd already managed to evade the hangman's noose three times in his life, and twice managed to somehow walk away with his life after finding himself eight paces from a firing squad with all barrels aiming at his head. And he was healthy as a horse. You have to be born under a lucky star – that's what it was. It was not for nothing that his associates liked to borrow something from him before going out on some excursion – a cap, a pair of old trousers, or even a handkerchief, 'for good luck'. Though an unscrupulous rogue, he must have had some kind of *inkluz*,[1] for he always emerged from any troublesome situation unscathed. He was a bandit, because that's what he was – a right and true bandit with a few dozen human lives on his conscience ... Ha, ha, ha! On his conscience! ... But he had been born under a lucky star and had an *inkluz*, there was no doubt about it. He raised his head defiantly and let out a whistle.

'I'll be all right! Long as I've got my health! Even if I have to swim my way out of this rain, damn it!'

He yanked his foot out of a ditch, shook off the mud, lifted it up, then struck it against some obstacle. He could hear plaster crumbling amid the pattering of rain.

'A hut?'

Carefully, he reached out his hand and felt the wall before him.

'Hey now! Just like that, a roof to lie under. Let's find the door!'

Sliding his hand along the wall, he walked around the corner and felt glass beneath his fingers. The cottage must have been small and squat, because just beyond the window the wall broke off again, and Żębroń, who was tall and sturdy as an oak, kept hitting his head on the straw eaves. Finally along the third face of the building he found the door and pounded his fist on it. It gave way meekly and let him in. Kuźma reached out his arms to the right, and then to the left, but felt only empty space.

'Aha! No entryway, just one stinkin' room. Speaking of ... what is that stench? Smells like death!' He spat in disgust. 'Well, better the stench and smoke than shivering my ass off in the rain. Hey! Is anyone here?'

The question seeped into the darkness ... He pulled out a pack of matches from his vest, took one out, and struck it. It failed to light. The second, the third, and the fourth failed in turn.

'Goddamn it! Bastards got soggy.'

---

1 According to one folk tradition, an *inkluz* was a magical coin that would always return to its owner, multiplying his riches; to obtain it, one had to sell his soul to the devil. It is unclear from the text whether the author is referring to Żębroń's possessing such a coin or if he is using the term more broadly to refer to a kind of protecting spirit. [Translator's note.]

He threw the box with such fury that it bounced off a wall and fell rustling to the floor.

'Looks like I'm stuck in this dump until dawn.' He sighed with resignation and started creeping blindly along the wall to the right of the entrance.

He soon came upon some men's clothes and underwear hanging on pegs. So someone did live here.

'Hey! Let me ask again,' Żebroń shouted at the top of his lungs. 'Is anyone here, damn it? Speak up, you bastard! Don't be afraid, I won't do anything to you. Are these your clothes?'

He strained his ears, held his breath, and waited. In vain. There was not even the slightest sound to indicate the presence of another person.

'Maybe he went out and will be back any moment. I'm not going to wait, anyway; I'm changing into these clothes. I'm freezing cold in these wet rags.'

He unbuckled his wide leather belt and folded it in four, took out a bulging purse and an equally stuffed wallet from his pocket and tied them all together tightly into a bundle with string. Then he gripped it in his teeth, unwilling to part with it even for a moment. It was the spoils of a decade's worth of criminal dealings and held the whole substance and meaning of his life.

He quickly threw off his soaked clothes and underwear and changed into the dry ones he'd found on the wall. A blissful feeling of warmth immediately spread over his body. He kicked away the discarded clothes with contempt, put his belt back on, stuffed his purse and wallet back into his pockets, and walked further into the room.

'I wonder,' he thought, 'what time it could be. Got to be after midnight. Closer to morning, hopefully. Damn, is it dark. Oh well, to hell with it!'

He bumped his knee against a bench, and at the same time felt a table stretching out before him. He took a seat. Only then did he feel the full weight of his exhaustion. He wouldn't have moved from that royally hospitable bench for anything in the world. He stretched his legs out before him and rested his elbows on the table. Now his stomach started talking; he was hungry as a wolf. It had been more than twenty-four hours since he'd last had anything to eat. There might be something to eat here, but how to find it in this damned darkness?

He banged his fist on the table and heard the tinkling of glass. Maybe that was his answer? Feeling around the surface of the table, his fingers met a glass, a wooden spoon, and a bowl. He lifted the dish to his nose . . . Smoked meat and cabbage. Fantastic!

Eagerly he dunked the spoon into the food and began to satisfy this most primal of urges. The dish was tasty, ample, and, most surprisingly, still warm. Someone must have prepared it just prior to his arrival, or stopped eating it only a moment before. For the first time in his life, Żebroń felt a deep sense of gratitude.

'To your health, you old boar!' he said exultantly.

He tilted the glass up to his mouth and wet his lips to taste it.

'Beer!'

He tossed it back in one gulp.

'Maybe there's a bottle here?'

A meticulous search of the table yielded negative results.

'Ha, tough luck. This'll have to do.'

He wiped his mouth with the sleeve of the kaftan he had thrown on, sat astride the bench and fell into a reverie. Although he badly wanted to sleep, he couldn't bring himself to get up and seek out a bed . . .

Yes, yes . . . He had damn good luck, real brigand's luck. Today was just another example of that. On such a nasty night, to find refuge in some mud hut in a clear field out in the middle of nowhere. Look at that! And what a refuge! With a change of clothes, supper, and beer!

He was born under a lucky star, that's all there was to it. Anyone else in his place would have bitten the dust long ago, but he, Żebroń the Red, still lived – going on almost forty years now, bringing glory to himself, terror to the people, and perpetual frustration to police, gendarmes, and plainclothesmen. Of his entire gang, only he – the ringleader – remained alive. All had perished, one by one, two by two, three by three – one here, one there, in various circumstances. He had lost them somewhere along the path of his brigand's life, like potatoes falling off the cart of a peasant boy who's loaded them up too carelessly. All healthy, reliable, charming men, he had let them be slaughtered like livestock. Twenty men! Twenty peasants as strong as oxen! They went out, they died, they disappeared without a trace . . .

The last two, Hapiak and Wakarski, were hanged on the gallows two weeks ago for murdering a factory owner while on a job with him. They had been sniffed out by intelligence officers, while he, Żębroń, had managed to escape. For three weeks he had been running away from the scene of the crime – first by train, then by carriage, and finally on foot. Today, he was totally safe. No one could do anything to him now; he'd been over the border since yesterday morning, carrying the passport of a man who had died under mysterious circumstances. His name, now, was Mikai Marinescu, and he was a Romanian subject. He had completely thrown off his pursuers, leading them in a northwesterly direction while he was sneaking past the southeastern borders of the country. Before they died, his two accomplices had tried to sell him out, giving the authorities a thorough description of him. This hadn't helped them, nor did it hurt him. They had no chance of finding him here; he had erased all traces of himself, changed his outfits numerous times, grown a hermit's beard. Besides, he was already abroad, somewhere on the Bessarabian plains . . .

Now he would start a new life – one marked by peace, stability, and safety. He was due for it now. Forty years old – 'the fourth cross on his back', as they say. Enough robbery, enough bloodshed. He needed to rest. His purse was well-stocked because he had always been thrifty, never spending 'blood-earned' money unnecessarily. And of course there was Ileana. He had met her at a bar in Warsaw, just a week before his last 'job'. Even then, he knew that it would be his last . . . She had been awaiting him for a month now in Iaşi. A loyal girl, not some hussy. Romanian. He had introduced himself to her as a fellow countryman, a sales agent from Bucharest. He could speak like a native Romanian, owing to his extensive dealings with smugglers in the mountains along the border. They got engaged. He gave her money for the journey and sent her back to her homeland, promising to follow her in a month. And he had kept his word. In a day or two, he would reach Iaşi and they would be married. Like decent people, in a church, the godly way. ha, ha, ha! The godly way . . . And they would be happy . . .

Why shouldn't they be? Anything was possible in this stupid world. You've just got to have a head on your shoulders, and your *inkluz*, which brings luck. *Inkluz,* or the devil; he rules the world, it's all the same. Just not God. If God ruled, he would not allow a brute such as himself to keep roaming around in it – a multiple murderer, deserter, thief, swindler, and overall bum. He himself, Kuźma Żębroń the Red, had been surprised more than once by his good fortune and could not reconcile it with his sense of justice, which was off wandering somewhere in the far corners of his lost soul. And now he was no longer afraid of anything, since even his last crime went unpunished. He wasn't even afraid of God Himself, for he did not believe in Him. There was only the devil, and his *inkluz*.

'Ha, ha, ha!' He finished his ruminations out loud. 'What are you gonna do to me? Ha, ha, ha.'

'Ha, ha, ha!' answered an echo.

'What's that?'

He raised his sleepy head and listened.

'What was that cackling?'

The perfect silence of the night and its deepening darkness calmed his nerves entirely.

'It's your own laughter, you dunce,' he reasoned to himself, and soon fell asleep . . .

At some point, a figure emerged from the haze of sleep – his beloved, framed against the background of a cherry orchard. She was walking towards him, young and comely, looking beautiful in her traditional Romanian dress. Ileana! . . . She threw her arms around his neck and offered her lips. He pressed his own against them . . . But . . . Whose lips were these? Whose foul breath? What's wrong with you, girl?! Get away from me, you cursed witch!

In his sleep, Żębroń's hands were violently pushing away someone's arms, tearing someone's mouth away from his lips, a mouth that was sinking its teeth into them . . .

He panted as he overcame the phantasm, and woke up . . .

He was still sitting on the bench with his body halfway turned toward the window, whose rectangle shone with a pale light against the graying dawn.

'The sun is rising.'

Slowly, he turned to face the room's interior. His still-drowsy gaze settled languidly on the outline of a bed opposite him, just a few steps away. On this bed, under a blanket, a man was lying on his side with his head propped up on his elbow, looking at him. He was watching with intense curiosity, as though waiting for something. Żebroń rubbed his eyes, became fully alert, and strained his eyes to stare at his host. He could not quite see the man's face in the semi-darkness, but slowly he began to make out the details. And the other man opened his large, spongy, artificial-looking mouth in a strange smile and spoke in a steady, monotonous voice, like rain rumbling through a gutter in foul weather:

'You are wearing my shirt and clothes.'

Żebroń did not quite grasp the meaning of these words, but he noticed that his host's lips were two horrifically festering rolls of rotten meat that reeked of blood and carrion.

'You ate what was left of my food with my spoon, and drank from my glass,' he rumbled, unrelenting. 'And when you fell asleep, I gave you a brotherly kiss. We're pals now, till the end of days.'

A face emerged from the half-shadow – a face full of wounds, without a nose, without eyebrows, without ears, followed by a scaly hand, with toxic bits of skin flaking off like sawdust . . .

A bovine roar erupted from Żebroń's throat, and he jumped off the bench.

'Don't touch me, or I'll gut you like a pig!'

'Ha, ha, ha! You're mine anyway, buddy. We are brothers from now on,' answered the wretched man.

'You lie, you mangy dog!'

'I am your leprous brother.'

Żebroń let out a stream of vile curses as he fled the room. Gnashing his teeth in horror, he cast off the robe, shirt and trousers and continued running into the boundless empty fields, huge and naked like Adam, the first man. All the while from behind, through the gloom of daybreak, the leaden gray of the burgeoning dawn, that wild, mocking laughter pursued him:

'Ha, ha, ha! You can't run away, you can't run away! I'll catch up – if not today, then tomorrow – if not tomorrow, then in a year, in two . . . Ha, ha, ha! Ha, ha, ha!'

And Kuźma Żębroń the Red knew that this time, he would not escape.

Red Magda

A midnight silence reigned at the fire station. A lantern hanging from a hook in the ceiling cast a dim spectrum of rays over the square room, with its two couches against the wall, file cabinet, and spare helmets. Two firemen sat at the table by the window over a game of checkers, occasionally puffing clouds of yellow smoke from long cherry pipes. They played without apparent interest, just to kill time, their hands moving lazily, as though unwilling, their faces looking bored and weary from their vigil. At times, one would give a wide yawn and stretch his back, hunched from overwork, or mutter some indistinct remark. Then silence would reign again, shrouded in pipe smoke.

On the couches lay the two men on duty; the one by the left wall was snoring heartily in an octave of tones, while his partner on the opposite side smoked a cigarette in silence, his eyes fixed on the ceiling. At some point he tore his eyes away from it, stubbed out the dying butt and tossed it into a corner. One of the players turned round:

'Not sleeping, sergeant?'

'For some reason I can't. Carry on with your game. I prefer to think a bit.' He stretched out again on the bed, clasped his hands under his head and gazed thoughtfully at a large image of St. Florian hanging on the wall. His thoughts were evidently troublesome, as his face kept clouding over, and every now and then he would draw the long black arches of his eyebrows together in discomfort.

The fire sergeant, Piotr Szponar, did in fact have something to worry about. Three weeks ago, his only child, Magda, had returned to domestic service in the town, and with her the same cares and concerns that had forced him two years earlier to send her somewhere far away, where no one had yet heard anything about her.

And the fireman's daughter was a strange creature. Tall, delicate, and pale, she attracted attention with her large black eyes, always staring off into space, and with the movements of her hands, which she was never quite able to control. These hands, as pale as her face, were constantly beset by a nervous trembling or cramping, causing spasmodic movements of the fingers – long, slender, and perpetually cold. She had abundant black hair with a lustrous, raven-like sheen whose coils always spilled out of her flame-colored silk shawl, the only accessory the poor girl could afford.

For the fireman's daughter was very poor indeed. Her mother, Marta, supposedly a gypsy of great beauty, had died young, bequeathing to her daughter a somewhat sickly, unusual nature and a longing for the vast, boundless steppes. Magda's father loved her with tender and sincere affection, albeit with a tinge of apprehension toward his own child. Piotr Szponar was afraid of his daughter. He was afraid of her face, as white as marble; of her narrow, tense mouth; of her frequent, long reveries. But there were also other, deeper reasons for his apprehension.

While his wife was still leading a nomadic life among her own people, an old gypsy woman had foretold that a white townsman would seduce her and that she would bear him a child – a girl, a daughter of the flames, against whom her father would fight all his life.

The fortune seemed to have strangely been fulfilled. Marta only lived to see the first part of it, having departed this world forever when the child was only five. Piotr waited anxiously for the realization of the second part, whose import was obscure to him at first. Then came the time when the witch's mysterious words began to assume their proper meaning. Magda Szponarówna was fifteen years old at the time, and was employed in town at the rolling-paper factory when the first fire broke out: for reasons unknown, the crates holding the paper sheets ignited, and the flames spread throughout the whole factory within a few minutes. It was an enormous loss, and the perpetrator was never discovered.

However, after the fire was extinguished, Magda was found in the small central hall sprawled on the floor in a deep sleep, having been spared by the sea of flames. The girl had probably endured the entirety of the fire in this state, and only when they had spent two hours trying to revive her did she open her sleep-heavy eyelids. How she had managed to survive for an hour without suffocating in a closed room surrounded on all sides by waves of flame, and how the room, situated in the middle of a burning building, survived at all – forever remained a mystery.

After this incident, Magda changed employers several times, usually serving as a maid for wealthier families, a café cloakroom attendant, or a shopgirl. And always by some fateful coincidence, shortly after she had assumed the position a fire would break out in the house or institution where she was working at the time. In each case, the cause of the disaster remained undetermined, and those involved found themselves confronted with a *fait accompli*.

At first, no one even dreamt of looking for a connection between the blazes and Magdalena Szponarówna, whose proper and irreproachable behavior did not draw anyone's attention. But eventually odd rumors began to circulate among the ranks of the town's proletariat concerning the recent, frequent conflagrations. For it transpired that there were sometimes two or even three fires a week, and – strangely enough – always in the same place; the fire seemed to take a liking to certain districts, and moreover, to certain houses and families, haunting them in a particularly intrusive manner. Finally, out of the blue, after a ferocious blaze in Lewandówka which almost completely destroyed the newly constructed home of the municipal clerk, a rumor spread that the cause of these disasters was none other than Magda Szponarówna, a servant in the Doleżan household. An angry mob of townsfolk attacked her in the middle of the market square and would have carried out a summary execution of the unfortunate girl if not for the intervention of her father, universally liked and respected as a defender of the public good, and the police, who carted the girl off before the mob could exact its vengeance.

The investigation, which was conducted very strictly and rigorously, did not establish the guilt of the defendant; on the basis of the testimony of witnesses as well as the accused, the examining magistrate was only able to conclude that, to everyone's astonishment, there had been more than a hundred fires in the town within just under a year of her having first taken employment, with these primarily occurring only in the homes of those whom she was serving at any given time. Moreover, a remarkable fact was established about Magda's behavior during the suspicious fires: in fifty out of the hundred cases, she was found in an unconscious, almost cataleptic state after the fire had been extinguished, usually inside the house where the incident had occurred. That was all. The prosecution was not able to provide evidence of direct guilt in any of the cases; at no point did anyone catch the accused in the act. Arson, in fact, seemed out of the question since, according to the testimony of eyewitnesses and victims, the girl would sit motionless, as if in a trance, from the moment the fire broke out until it was extinguished; moreover, the fires did not start in her immediate vicinity, but usually at a distance of some two or three rooms away.

Several expert physicians showed a keen interest in the matter and, after thoroughly examining Magda, pronounced her to be an abnormal creature with a predominance of subconscious forces, prone to catalepsy and even somnambulism.

Finally a verdict of not guilty was reached, but the court confidentially advised the fire sergeant not to seek further employment for his Magda, since public opinion was strongly against her. Despite her acquittal, the girl, nicknamed 'Red Magda', was regarded as an arsonist and a witch, whom everyone avoided, fearing to admit her into their homes.

Her anguished father sent her away to relatives in the countryside in the hope that she would be able to return after some time, when public recollection of the catastrophes had faded, and people had forgotten about Red Magda.

And so she spent two years living in the village, without giving any sign of her existence. Then, three weeks ago, she had suddenly come back to town looking paler than usual, with sunken cheeks and traces of tears in her reddened eyes. She answered questions reluctantly, clearly out of compulsion, and was only eager to find employment so as not to be a burden on her father at home. Finally, he gave in to her persistent entreaties and, though with a heavy heart, arranged a position for her in the house of one Duchnic, a wealthy merchant, on Młynarska Street. The girl assumed the role of a maid there, and within a week was already performing her duties diligently.

The reappearance of Red Magda in town somehow failed to cause a stir, as no one seemed to take notice of the fact. But Piotr Szponar was worried sick over her return and waited anxiously each day for the 'bad news'. For, despite the court's verdict and Magda's own categorical denial of guilt, he did not believe in her innocence; somewhere deep down, at the very bottom of his soul, slumbered the conviction that everything people had said about her reflected a sad and terrible truth. As both her father and sergeant of the fire department, he was qualified to have an opinion on this – he, who had by his own hand extinguished all of the fires which popular opinion had connected in a mysterious way to his Magda. He had had time to recognize all of the accompanying signs and to examine them in exacting detail, to distinguish them using his own individual sense from the 'typical' ones with which he was also deeply familiar. It was not for nothing that he had attained the rank of sergeant and was considered a first-rate firefighter. If he were asked in the confession booth, 'Fire Sergeant Piotr Szponar – is your daughter guilty?', he would answer no, as far as her own conscience and all the known facts were concerned. But if someone were to ask him if he believed unequivocally in Magda's innocence, he would be just as emphatic in his denials.

But what pained him most was that this was his daughter, his own flesh and blood. There was a kind of painful irony in the fact that his own child seemed to be generating around her the same destructive force that he had been fiercely eradicating for so many years. Sometimes the strange thought occurred to him that perhaps it was precisely because of the tenacity with which he had been fighting against fire that he had been visited by this scourge; perhaps the cruel element was taking its revenge against him in this way? There was no way of knowing. His thoughts wandered in this manner, and he suffered greatly.

Even now, at this late hour, he could find no refuge from his anxious thoughts, which roamed hither and thither like phantoms inside his skull.

He lifted himself with some effort from the couch and, attempting to distract his tormented mind, began to look over the list of emergency procedures pasted on the wall. But soon this too became tiresome and, looking bored, he turned to the blackboard on which duties were written and began to draw a caricature in chalk.

Suddenly, the silence was shattered by the sound of a bell: three sharp, piercing clangs. The fire alarms were going off.

Motion broke out in the guards' tower, figures flitting to and fro past the windows. His heart pounding, Szponar studied the output of the telegraph. Every moment brought him new details, precise to the minute, to the second. The fireman's eyes were fixed on the luminous platinum dial, and then he shut them. Just as a nervous card player keeps his cards under his hand, guessing at what they may be before turning them over – so he covered his eyes for fear of facing the truth. At last he opened them and stared intently at the output. Here was the answer before him: direct, concise and inexorable.

'Hurry! District 9. Garbarze. Młynarska Street.'

Szponar swayed on his feet and went pale. His intuition had not deceived him. Yes – there it was – without a doubt! Where else? Of course the fire would be at the Duchnic residence! The calvary of fires was starting all over again. Already, in her third week of service! The rush of pain and disbelief at the fact doubled him over for a moment, but he took hold of himself. There was no time to think; it was necessary to act, to give orders, to assume command.

Already the trumpet was sounding the alarm, summoning the emergency services; already the fire crew, who had been snoozing just moments before, were hurriedly fastening their gear, putting on their helmets, throwing coils of rope and rescue harnesses over their backs.

The sergeant ran out of the firehouse into the courtyard. Here, beneath the climbing wall and in the storehouse, preparations for departure were feverishly under way. The wooden double-doors

were thrown open and a pair of fire engines were rolled out, along
with a supply car and a couple of balaclavas for the exclusive use
of the crew. Under the glare of the headlights, their metal helmets
shone, and their ax blades glimmered icily.

Szponar, now calm and level-headed, gave orders. His voice –
steady, confident, virile – reverberated in the courtyard.

'Are the valves in order?' he asked at one point.

A pair of obedient arms reached in toward the pistons of the
steam pumpers and examined them.

'Sergeant, I report that the valves are functional,' announced
one of the men.

'Good. Listen up, boys!' he shouted, taking up a position on
one of the wagons. 'It's time to hit the road! Godspeed, let's go!'

The resonant blare of the Ace trumpet sounded, and both
panels of the exit gate were flung open; amid the hubbub of sirens
and the crimson light of burning torches, the firemen's wagons
clambered out into the quiet street. The supply car sped out ahead,
followed by another car loaded with ladders, pitchforks, pick-
axes and fire-flappers along with a huge water tank, and then two
'Matador'-type fire engines with their operators, and finally, the
passenger car with a crew under the command of Sgt. Szponar . . .

It was three in the morning on a dead November night. A violent wind was blowing in from the valleys on either side of the
street, kicking up sand and cobblestone dust into everyone's eyes.
Yellow tufts of autumn leaves blew here and there from gardens,
racing over the sidewalk slabs with a dry rustle.

They passed Aleje and turned into Świętojańska Street. Far
away, from over the towers of the parish church, the orange glow
of the blaze could be seen. Frightened faces peered from windows,
sleepy watchmen appeared at gates; groups of people began to
gather in public squares.

And in the empty streets, elongated by lantern light cast over
the frontages, loud, boisterous sounds reverberated; the call of fire
horns, the metallic sound of the trumpet.

'Hurry! Hurry!'

They reached Holy Spirit Square. Blood-red bursts of flame
shot up from behind the dark outlines of tenement houses, with

smoke billowing up in black, lugubrious coils. Already they could smell the stench of burning in the air, hear the rising din of shouts and screams . . .

They passed the square, shot around the post office and rushed full-speed into Młynarska Street. Further down on the left, their eyes were struck by a formidable blaze; the three-story home of the merchant Duchnic was in flames. The fire, which had broken out on the second floor, continuously fanned by the gusty autumn winds, had engulfed the upper floors within a quarter of an hour and was now extending purple ribbons down toward the ground floor. Despite the late hour, everything around was bright as day. Amidst the screams of people and the crackling of the flames, the emergency vehicles rushed into the large square in front of the building, which at that moment was strewn with bits of flaming material. They were greeted by sounds of turmoil and torment. In the street around the house lay heaps of furnishings thrown from the rooms, whole piles of trunks, wardrobes, and woven carpets all heaped in a chaotic jumble.

The fire had broken out so suddenly and spread so quickly that many people had only managed to escape in their undergarments. Others had had their exit path cut off by flames erupting from the lower floors and remained in the burning house, waiting for help to arrive. Every now and then one could spot the pale faces of these unfortunate ones in the windows, vainly begging for a rescue which had yet to come. One woman, driven to despair by the delay, had thrown herself from the third floor onto the pavement and died on the spot. It was at this critical moment that the firemen arrived. In a flash, the gawkers were cleared from the street and a line of hoses was laid from the house to the bank of the neighboring river. Before the rubber trunks had drawn enough water into the tank, the powerful extinguishers began their work. The noble 'Rese' and 'Matador' units, vigorously fed by manual hydrophones, blasted streams of water at the most concentrated area of fire: the second and ground floors. Simultaneously, five extension ladders and two hook ladders were secured to the building. Lifting the hose nozzle high up with his right hand, Sergeant Szponar was the first to climb the rungs.

'Follow me, boys!' he encouraged his companions in a thunderous voice.

Galvanized by his example, six more firemen began to ascend the ladders towards the threatened floors; outlet hoses slithered behind them, fastened to ledges and rungs on the way up. Having reached the second floor, Szponar unleashed a strong, concentrated current of water into the apartment opposite, in which dense pockets of fire and smoke were swirling. The red whirlpool momentarily collapsed and receded further into the structure, revealing the interior of a room half-stripped of furnishings.

'They must have all escaped from here,' he concluded. And he left the care of the second floor to his two colleagues who had caught up with him in the meantime.

Since the ladder did not extend higher, he hooked himself with a carabiner to its penultimate rung at waist level, grabbed the hook ladder given to him from below by his colleague in both hands and, raising it high above his head, swiftly hooked it onto the sill of a third-story window. He executed this maneuver with fabulous skill and speed and began to climb up the rungs, gripping an ax in his right hand.

Having consumed and devastated the two lower levels, the bloody mane of flames now stretched up to the third; long, fiery tongues lapped at the balconies and porches; red stingers penetrated the doors and windows. Human screams rang out, mingled with the sound of shattering glass.

On one of the balconies, a dozen or so residents were huddled in a group, shielding themselves with their hands from the heat of the rapidly approaching flames.

At that moment, the sergeant reached their level. In a single swift motion, he reached for the nearest woman, lifted her just over the balcony railing as her hair billowed in the wind, and handed her to his companion below, who brought her down as she swooned in his arms.

'The rescue net!' ordered Szponar, seeing that the group on the balcony was growing, and that the fire had already entered the interior.

Having saved a few more people in this way, he entrusted the rest to his colleagues, leaving for himself the most difficult task of plunging inside the burning house. He adjusted his smoke hood, unfastened the carabiner, straddled the uppermost rung of the ladder and jumped in through the window. The treacherous flames slithered in behind him.

And so the fireman commenced his heroic task. Like a diver at the bottom of the sea, Szponar threw himself in all directions in a feverish search, racing through quiet, lavishly decorated boudoirs, anxiously traversing recently abandoned bedrooms. Suddenly, he came across a body lying on the floor. He bent down, lifted it up and, amidst clouds of suffocating smoke, turned back toward the window. Here, fortunately, he came upon one of his men and handed over his burden: a pretty girl about ten years old.

'Attach the emergency chutes to the top two floors!' he shouted, before turning back and rushing into the side wing of the house.

At that moment, the unvanquished fire had seized the left side of the third story and was pressing its burning lava into the very heart of the building. The sergeant turned for an instant to see a thin, purplish column of flame rising out of an alcove. He took in a sniff of the air and detected a scent that he knew very well – her hair.

This was not the first time he had encountered this scent during a fire: the flames smelled of thyme and walnut leaves – the same decoctions with which Magda so keenly washed her long black hair.

There was no doubt: this was her fire.

As if driven by fury, he rushed toward a narrow corridor on the right from which moans could be heard. But right at the mouth of it, the red specter of a young woman stood in his way. She was taller than humanly possible, monstrously exaggerated in size, and was shaking a bundle of flames clutched in her hand.

He shielded himself from her with an outstretched arm and, trembling all over, asked hoarsely:

'What do you want from me?'

In response, a cruel smile played on her lips and a stream of fire ran over her flaming cheeks. She raised the bundle of flames and blocked the passage with it.

'Out of my way!' he shouted, wild with fear and rage. 'Get out of the way, Magda!'

And he passed through her as through a purple mist. Something scorched him so badly on his arms and neck that he hissed with pain, but he managed to break through.

A moment later, he was carrying an old woman in his arms and, straddling the windowsill, he handed her to one of the firemen on the ladder.

Meanwhile, others lowered the residents onto the nets, or, in the case of the more robust ones, men in particular, in rescue chairs hastily secured by ropes and cords; some of the bolder ones jumped straight onto the blankets spread out below. Only the top floor remained. Despite the firemen's efforts, the blaze, fueled by a hellish wind, had already engulfed the entire house and was stretching triumphantly above the roof.

Szponar gave his best effort, rushing about in all directions. Like a demon of salvation he charged into the densest areas of flame, hovering over the abyss with utter disregard for his own life, poised at every moment between heaven and earth like a tightrope walker. He managed to carry twenty people out with his own two hands, save the lives of two of his colleagues, and secure the return of several others. But amid all this, the specter of the red wench never ceased to plague him, to irritate him with the smell of her fiery hair. Here, her face emerged from a nebula of smoke; there, her bloody figure flitted past as the porch collapsed behind her, her infernal locks giving off showers of sparks.

He paid no heed to any of this and, armored in the steel of an iron will, fulfilled his duties heroically. And then came the moment for the most terrible trial of all.

There was no question of saving the house; the scorched beams of the upper floors were giving way and crashing down on the floors below, the pockmarked ceilings caving in with a deafening rumble. A small group of fourth-floor residents was huddled in one of the windows on the right wing of the building, which was now partially engulfed by flames: two old men, a sick invalid, and a young mother with a baby at her breast.

The firemen, led by the sergeant, hurriedly attached an emergency chute that would help them lower the most infirm to the ground below.

Suddenly, the woman in the window broke into frantic screaming. Holding the crying child with her left arm, she pointed with her other hand to the churning wall of flames approaching with frightening rapidity from the depths of the room. Yellow coils of acrid smoke momentarily concealed the unfortunate group.

When seconds later the wind pushed aside this suffocating veil, Szponar was met with a bloodcurdling image.

Through the window he could see Red Magda bending with serpentine flexibility, trying to set fire to the already deployed rescue chute with the bundle of flames in her hand. A satanic smile played on the girl's lips, infernal joy lit up her face, encircled with a halo of fiery hair. The maleficent barb of flame crept ever closer to the canvas . . .

'Jesus, Mary!' Szponar groaned. 'Die, monster!'

He made the sign of the cross in the air, then flung the hatchet at her.

The blade smashed into her forehead. There was a horrible howl, followed by a long, drawn-out wail.

The red specter quickly retreated into the house and vanished in the flames.

The sergeant ran a hand over his forehead and looked around in a daze. Something in him suddenly cracked, and he no longer had the strength to go on. His comrades came to assist him.

The fire abruptly dimmed, shrank, receded; the pumps took the upper hand at last. Amidst the spray of water gushing from their maws, the final residents were carefully lowered to the ground.

The sky had turned gray by the time the firemen, deathly exhausted and black from soot and smoke, descended the ladders to the street. Sergeant Piotr Szponar rounded out the procession with staggering steps . . .

All of a sudden there was shouting. From among the crowd gathered outside the scorched house, the horrible name could be heard:

'Red Magda! Red Magda!'

He forced his way in among them.

'Move aside! Move aside! I'm her father!' And he made his way between the long, vexatious rows of onlookers up to the charred entrance gate of the building.

The fireman staggered past them like a drunk, being pelted by their stares, and turned mechanically to the left, toward a small area of the house that had miraculously escaped the fire. On a shabby bunk in the corner of a room, he saw his daughter's corpse lying in a pool of blood; black, partially clotted blood still oozed from her savagely smashed skull.

'Magda! My Magda!' he croaked, his voice inhuman.

And he slumped unconscious against the wall.

The Loft

It was a Sunday afternoon. The hot August sun beat down on the rooftops, and the stifling heat slumbered in the recesses of the tenement houses.

Three o'clock, the leisurely hour just after lunch. Blinds or canvas shades were drawn over all the windows, cutting off the interior from the solar orgy outside. All motion in the stairwells had ceased, all bustle in the street deadened. Only servants could be seen, feverishly preparing for the Sunday amusements. From time to time figures of young women appeared on porches, hurrying with buckets to the sinks or waste bins, red-faced from rushing and impatient with the work that was delaying their evening freedom. In half an hour the parish church bells would ring for vespers, just the time to finish up the dishes and finally escape the stuffy kitchen air . . .

In the courtyard near the well, a watchman stretched out on a faded straw mattress, dozing in the warm sun. Beside him an old mongrel dog, a pitch-black Gypsy, dragged its wasted body into the guardhouse, panting with its tongue hanging out. A couple of hens pecked lazily among the ferns . . .

On the balcony, in a recess between the second-floor walls, fourteen-year-old Wisia was sitting on a chair. Her fiery black eyes plunged restlessly into the dark neck of the opposite corridor, then looked up again to the hall window.

Wisia was waiting. With an impatient movement of her plump little hand, she brushed a cascade of ebony-black hair behind her ear and listened for the sound of footsteps. After a moment, she shook her head in disappointment.

It wasn't Grześ. That good-for-nothing! He was supposed to come right after lunch, and it was already past three and he hadn't shown. She'd been in such a hurry to eat her pudding that her mother noticed and asked why. She had lied then, saying she had to finish a book that she was to return to her girlfriend tomorrow. She had lied for him, so that she would not be late for her tryst, but he . . .

Wisia felt a strange tightness in her throat, as though she were about to cry. This infuriated her. No! She would not cry! She would rather go back to her room and not show herself to that scoundrel for a whole week.

She sprang from her seat to fulfill this intention, but her legs would not obey. She suddenly felt rather listless.

Maybe he couldn't shake his parents? Maybe he was doing those boring lessons with that teacher again? She would have to wait a bit longer.

She leaned with her back against the wall and stretched out her legs toward the sun. A stream of sunlight washed over her bare calves and tickled her knees. Wisia closed her eyes in pleasure. Just as though Grześ were kissing her. He always had such warm lips. Such sweet, powerful lips! And how sweetly he always looked at her, how deep, deep into her eyes, taking her breath away, making her act strangely, so very strangely . . . Grześ, my dearest! Nicer than mother, than father, than anyone else in the world! How he always kissed her, cuddled her, caressed her . . .

They had met on the balcony a year ago. She was reading as usual in her corner when he too came out with a book and leaned on the balustrade a few steps away from her. They didn't speak to each other then; he just stared at her the whole time, then bowed in farewell. From then on, they saw each other daily at the same time and talked in hushed voices about various subjects.

They still had not kissed yet, being too self-conscious. On the balcony, someone might see them from the windows. It was only a few months later that he kissed her. Wisia was always overcome with passion when she reflected on that first kiss. She remembered exactly how it had played out. Grześ stood as usual by her little nook, and after a few words of greeting he whispered in low tones:

'Come into the hallway with me.'

'No way. What if someone sees us?' she protested feebly.

'Nobody will,' he assured her. 'I'll go in first, as though going back to my place, and I'll wait for you there. Just sit here for a bit and then follow me. No one will notice. We'll have a bit of fun, just for a little while. Really, just a very short while,' he added, looking pleadingly into her eyes. 'Wisia, darling, don't refuse!'

And Wisia went. She walked down that long, dark, endless corridor which always filled her with a curious dread whenever she looked into its dim, gloomy depths.

It was there that he kissed her for the first time. She remembered how she almost gave them away when she let out a cry of terror as he suddenly grabbed her in the darkness and pulled her close to him. It was terrible and sweet at the same time. No one noticed them because they immediately went off to their apartments afterward.

From then on, they met for a brief while every day in the black corridor. These were strange and mysterious moments for Wisia. An indefinable fear of the place, along with the idea of doing something forbidden, merged with the charm of her girlish desires into one marvelous tangle of feelings that rocked the whole of her sexually-awakened being with a painful intoxication. Her youthful, prematurely exuberant loveliness trembled ever more intensely as a dormant current of passion began to rage within her, arousing hot and sultry desires. Grześ knew how to sense them, and how to feed them. He devised various amusements for the two of them.

Before long, they began to regard the corridor as uncomfortable and potentially unsafe. It was time to find a better refuge.

Grześ noticed that the corridor, which was otherwise empty, terminated at the other end in a set of doors which were always closed, and which no one ever used. He also discovered that there were no apartments on the other side of the doors, only the rear wall of the tenement building exiting onto an empty courtyard. The building, already very old, had at one time apparently extended into that space, but when that entire wing collapsed due to a fire, the frugal landlord had opted to have the damaged wall leveled without bothering to rebuild the rest. The doors were left over from the old construction, a vestigial remnant of the former dwelling.

Cut in bizarre zigzags, and covered in countless drawings in chalk and coal, the outer doors rested only loosely in the hasp and stuck out past the molding. With just a few strokes of a file they swung open, revealing a spacious gap comprising the space between the interior and exterior doors.

This space became the sanctuary of their love. For their comfort, Grześ brought in an old, wobbly bench stolen from his parents' woodshed, propped its shorter leg up with a stone and covered it with a tattered kilim rug. It turned out to be a perfect hideaway, a place where no one could track them down.

Here, in absolute darkness, illuminated perhaps only by the light of his matches or the faint glow coming in from the half-open door, they experienced moments as fleeting as dreams, and just as marvelous. Here, in this cramped, constricted space, they became acquainted for the first time with the mysteries of touch, learned to appreciate the pleasures of carnal reciprocity.

By virtue of their repeated efforts, their creativity grew, and their range of possible enjoyments expanded; they exerted themselves in devising ever new ways of satisfying their desires, outdoing themselves in finesse and refinement. But they both sensed the inadequacy of their means and the perpetual hunger of dissatisfaction, which cannot be tricked into accepting a substitute. After these few brief moments they returned to their apartments aglow with passion, inflamed, insatiable, with a lust for the morrow which would bring new intensities, new sensations, and new disappointments . . .

The prior day's rendezvous had been shorter than usual. Grześ had dropped in only for a minute, and seemed in a hurry. As he was leaving, he said cryptically:

'I've found a new spot, somewhere even more comfortable. I also thought up a new game, something you haven't even dreamed of. But we couldn't do it here. There, on the other hand . . .'

She pressed her lips against his.

'Something even more pleasurable?' she whispered.

'Yes. I read about it in one of my father's books. Now I know how older people have fun. Tomorrow's Sunday, my parents have an engagement and are sending me off to the cinema. I'm going to take advantage of this absence, so we'll have a lot more time. You try to get free too. So? Will you come?'

'I'll come.'

She smiled, throwing her arms around his neck.

And so they parted. That night, Wisia's sleep was restless. She kept dreaming of a long dark passage, from the mouth of which a pair of thin hands reached out and tried to pull her inside. She fought with all her might and resisted the phantom in a desperate struggle; finally, exhausted by her efforts, she slipped into a bottomless pit and lost consciousness. She woke up late in the morning, tired and pale.

The morning dragged on with unbearable tedium. Her heart thumping, she had finished lunch and taken advantage of her mother's siesta to sneak out onto the porch and wait for him. But he was late. Wisia's impatience grew by the second, aroused by fear and curiosity. She got up and, tiptoeing past the line of windows, moved towards the door leading into the hallway . . .

Suddenly, she trembled. To her left she heard the careful creaking of a door and the turning of a key in a lock. Grześ was approaching – a lean boy of sixteen with soft, girlishly delicate features. Having quickly surveyed the porch and stairwell, his violet eyes, cast over with a light fog of pensiveness and lustful melancholy, finally fixed themselves firmly upon her. He took her warm, velvety hands in his and pulled her into the dark mouth of the hallway.

'Wiśka, my golden, dark-browed girl, have you come?' he whispered, passionately snuggling up to her.

And she was already offering him her moist, cherry-plump lips.

Treading softly and quietly, they reached the end of the dark hallway. Wisia grabbed the door handle, but Grześ stopped her.

'We're going somewhere else today. Have you really forgotten what I said yesterday? I found a better place.'

Wisia looked questioningly into his eyes.

'This way,' he said, indicating the broken staircase just to the right of the door, which was barely visible in the twilight.

'To the old loft?' she asked, instinctively recoiling in fear.

'Nobody's gone up there for years. The steps are all worn out and rotted.'

'Don't be scared, Wiśka. They're safe to walk on. I've been up there and back a few times, not even one has bent under my foot. I got the key to the door – we'll go up there as though to our own bedroom.'

She hesitated.

'Something about it makes me afraid. It's so dark and scary there. I can't see the edges of the steps, we might trip going up.'

'Don't be a child,' he rebuked her impatiently. 'I've got a candle stub and matches. Anyway, we're going together; I'll help you up.'

She gave in silently. They began their ascent, Wisia in front and Grześ behind, lighting the way with his candle.

The stairs led straight up for a while, then turned right and disappeared into the darkness of the vaulted ceiling. The creeping candle flame conjured up strange shadows on the moldering walls, like huge, ludicrously threatening monsters. Frightened by their gestures, large, repulsive spiders scuttled obliquely across the walls.

The decaying steps creaked timidly in hushed protest, their rust-colored rot crumbling underfoot.

They passed the bend in the staircase and proceeded in a spiral to the top.

'Stop,' Grześ whispered. 'We're here. Let me step past you and open the door.'

He went up until his head touched the ceiling; the stairs terminated in an old-fashioned horizontal door. He took out a big rusty key and inserted it into the lock. After a couple of unsuccessful attempts, the bolt finally shot back.

'Hold this for a second!'

Handing her the candle end, he pushed against the trapdoor with arms extended, slowly raising it up. A draft came through the gap from the loft, extinguishing the flame.

'Grześ – where are you?'

'Here; give me your hand.'

She felt his warm, strong grip and went up a few steps. As Grześ continued to push, the door slowly swung from its horizontal position to a right angle from the floor.

The boy stood at the threshold and held the door up with his back, letting his companion pass through.

Wisia climbed unsteadily past the final step, sighing with relief as she reached the floor of the loft. Grześ grasped the edge of the door and carefully began to lower it.

'What a hideous door,' Wisia remarked. 'Almost ... predatory, with all those nails and hooks!'

Indeed, it looked downright malevolent. The whole of the longer, sliding batten which attached to the sides of the opening was outfitted at intervals with iron hooks that sunk like claws into the corresponding eyelets on the floor.

'Eh, who cares? Don't pay any attention to it.'

He bent down, straining to soften the impact of the fall, and fitted the door back into its original position.

'Now, a place of our own ...' he said, turning toward her with a strange glimmer in his eye. 'Wiśka, my Wiśka!'

He snuggled up to her, putting his arm around her lithe, virginal waist.

'My Grześ! Bright, sweet boy!' she whispered through parted lips.

And so they stood in silence for a long, delightful moment. Rays of afternoon sunlight coming in through chinks in the roof poured down in narrow streams, playing in warm colors on the girl's red blouse. Thick, dark billows of dust kicked up by their feet rose in the air, their myriad specks dancing in the light.

They looked out through one of the loft windows. Down below there stretched a sea of roofs, gables, domes and steeples, and the city hummed with the Sunday bustle.

'Pretty,' she said softly, resting her head on his shoulder.

'Come on,' he said, gently guiding her back into the room.

'Where to?' she asked as if in a dream, yielding to his will.

'There in the corner, between those two beams. I found an old, forgotten divan there. Very comfortable. All the springs are intact.'

In hushed voices, they exchanged expressions of affection in a tone of passionate cynicism, punctuated by shudders of increasing lust.

They sat on the divan. Gradually, amid an orgy of kisses, he eased her back toward the headboard and began to caress her legs.

She did not resist. Placing her arm behind her head, she closed her eyes and submitted to his frenzied hands. Their quiet intoxication was broken from time to time by short, childish words, unnecessary, humorously pointless questions, the suppressed murmuring of strained throats:

'You want it? Wiśka? . . . You want it? Do you feel . . .'

Suddenly she pulled him in towards her, wrapping her legs around him. A red mist blurred her vision. A scream, short and painful, resounded in the loft, then a second, a third . . . and then a quiet, prolonged sobbing . . .

Grześ pulled away and kneeled beside the divan, taking the girl's weeping face in both hands.

'Wisia! My dear, darling Wiśka! Does it hurt? Eh? A lot? My darling, please don't be angry with me!'

She sat up, smoothing out her ruffled dress. 'A bit,' she said, smiling through tears. 'But I'm all right now. My Grześ!'

She pressed his head to her chest.

'My sweet, golden boy!'

He lay his head in her lap and looked long and deep into her eyes. Suddenly she gave a start and, blanching, began listening for something.

'Do you hear that?' she whispered, trembling. 'Do you?'

'What?'

'Jesus! Maria!' she cried, rushing toward the exit. 'Hurry, open this door! That's my mother calling for me! You don't hear?'

He heard it now. From down below, a voice was clearly calling: 'Wisia! Wisia!'

With trembling hands, they both worked to unlatch the hooks and pull open the door. Grześ went down a few steps first, holding the door above their heads; Wisia lagged behind, stepping uncertainly down just past the edge of the opening. The boy leaned into the depths of the stairwell, straining to see in the darkness.

'Wisia! Where are you?' her mother continued to shout from below.

Grześ's outstretched hand trembled convulsively, and he carelessly let go of the door. Above him he felt a rush of air as the door fell, but he did not hear the impact of it falling into place against the floor.

'Wisia! Wisia!' called the voice, but it seemed further away now.

He started feeling around anxiously in the darkness.

'Wisia!' he whispered. 'Give me your hand. Where are you?'

The girl was silent.

'Wisia! What's wrong with you?'

He put a hand on her leg, which seemed to be kneeling on one of the steps above him. He took a step up, running his hand along her body, wondering whether she had fainted; he reached her neck, and his hand struck against the wood of the trapdoor. A terrible thought dawned in his mind ... He violently forced the door upward until it opened completely.

Light coming in through the loft illuminated the horrific scene.

Wisia was kneeling on the staircase with her head lying limply over the edge of the opening; the poor girl's neck was stuck between two of the floor-hooks, their iron claws driven into her neck by the force of the falling door. The blow was so forceful it must have crushed her vertebrae instantly. She died without so much as a groan ...

Evening had set in as the boy descended from the loft. He came down slowly and carefully, because in his arms he carried the precious burden of his dead beloved ...

Countess Maspera's Secret

The dinghy coasted ashore. It was welcomed into the protective arms of a secluded cove surrounded by a palisade of rocks. Moored with a rope to a basalt outcrop, the boat danced gently on the rippling waves. The turbulence of the open water had no access here; the sea, slithering in through a narrow gap between the reefs into the rock-ringed pool, was like a snake with its teeth removed – gentle now, and docile as a child.

This made its fanfare on the other side of the rocks, in the shallows, all the more menacing. The afternoon was stormy, for it was autumn.

Count Maspera took his wife's hand and helped her out of the boat. Her figure was outlined in a slender contour against the backdrop of stony gray. They followed a steep rocky path carved out of the basalt ridge which rose above the level of the bay. Then they stopped and, leaning against the edge of the cliff, bade farewell to the sea.

It was beautiful. Rippled and furrowed by the westerly breeze, it shook its locks menacingly like a disgruntled giant. Fractured rays of sunlight cast bloody hues upon the foam, while the silver underbellies of seagulls flashed by over the purple swell. In the boundless distance, as far as the eye could see, the rocking hips of the waves, bulging and spreading, spraying and receding – white eruptions of noise, like the crests of kalpaks, or the plumes on tritons' helmets – sometimes spurting up in bluish-green jets, sometimes rising in a cerulean wall and . . . emptiness – boundless emptiness, gilded with the coral smile of the sunset. Bożena nuzzled her head against her husband's breast.

'How beautiful, and how sad, Henry.'

And when he remained silent and only pressed her more tightly against him, she added:

'I love the poetry of this secluded space, so wild and forlorn. And you, Henry?'

'And I love it because it allows me to indulge in the pleasure of having you, Bożena, without any interruption. I love it because I know that here, no other man can look upon you, besides me; no eye full of desire will rest on you, save for mine.'

She gave him a melancholy look.

'Is your love for me, then, dominated by the senses?'

He leaned over her and kissed her on the lips.

'Hush, dearest! Do not blaspheme! I am your husband. Are you unhappy with me?'

'Let's go home now, Henry. It's getting late, and there's a chill coming off the sea.'

She wrapped her shawl around her. They walked in silence along the path that zigzagged among the rocks toward the castle. Dusk had fallen and the torches were already lit by the time they entered the courtyard and reached the front entrance gate. The old majordomo led them up the hill to the dining hall, holding a three-armed candelabra in his trembling hand.

After supper, Bożena sat down at the organ in the castle's bay window, which jutted out of the massive structure towards the sea. The cloudy October night, peeking in through the ogival windows, imparted a gloomy air; melodies of autumnal twilight floated up from under the fair-haired lady's fingers and drifted away. His head reclining on the armchair's headrest, Maspera admired her profile, as expressive as a cameo, followed the flowing movements of her hands over the keyboard and the wonderful lines of her slightly bent waist as she leaned into the notes. Watching her, he felt the fire within him burning anew, as he had every day for the past four years, since the day he had married this white daughter of the North and brought her with him to this seaside retreat, here to feast on her intoxicating beauty. And it seemed to him that her snowy body would be an inexhaustible source of pleasure for himself, and that, having once experienced the sweetness of her cool arms wrapped around his neck in a languorous embrace, he would never again desire the caress of any other.

Bożena was an ideal, the embodiment of everything he

yearned for and dreamt of in a woman: a perfect and utterly flaw-
less work of art. Maspera's love was the sensual passion of an artist
who loves the body but cannot see the soul that looks through it;
he did not seem to sense that Bożena owed half of her charm to
her inner beauty. There was something sacrilegious in his love.
The more strongly the spiritual aspect of her beauty asserted
itself, the more apparent the evidence of her extramundane
origin became, the more sensual desire she aroused in him. The
very thought that this sacred, pre-Raphaelite beauty was his wife,
whom he could possess whenever an amorous whim struck him,
sent him into a state of erotic intoxication bordering on orgasm.
The Count's caresses amounted to a kind of psychical sadism; he
felt diabolically sacrilegious as he brutally stripped bare this ven-
erated Madonna. Her imploring smile as she fought helplessly
against his rapacious lust drove him wild. In this conflagration of
his senses, their conjugal acts transformed into acts of rape and
desecration.

Bożena surrendered passively, putting up no resistance. She
regarded her husband's sensual caresses as symbolic in nature –
naïve, earthly equivalents of deeper, metaphysical feelings. In the
innermost secrets of her subtle soul, she looked upon his outbursts
as childish, innocent manifestations of a Southern European man's
affection, which he did not know how to express in any other
way. She loved the artist in him, the painter; she understood this
man of the South, descendant of conquistadors, in whose blood
the fires of the subtropical sun burned. She counted on the future,
on the influence she might exert upon him as the years wore on.
She expected the blaze of carnal rapture to burn out with time,
to become ennobled into a blue flame of adoration. Even as they
entwined her body, the red snakes of his passion did not manage
to invade and ignite her spiritual interior; she remained white and
pure, untouched by the kisses of this fiery simoom. Her love for
her husband was the color of a moonlit night . . .

This evening had put Bożena in a deeply lyrical mood. She
partook of the sadness of that great expanse of water. The 'song
without words' she conjured up on the organ was an expression
of that sadness. It wept with unfulfilled longings, the pain of dis-

appointment, the agony of autumn. These were echoed from out-side by the rhythmic churning of the sea and the moaning of the wind . . . Suddenly she felt his arms embrace her violently, lifting her up and cradling her like a child, his mouth panting with desire against her lips. Her lax body, resting indifferently on the otto-man, assumed a position of inertia, her eyes took refuge under the cover of heavy eyelids, her lips creased in a weary smile. A wave of bright, shimmering golden hair flowed from her head as it tilted over the edge of the bed. An arm whiter than snow slid languidly down.

Maspera took her in with predatory eyes. Shuddering all over, he began to sate himself on her priceless beauty . . .

An hour later, exhausted but triumphant, he walked away from the bed. Bożena raised her closed eyelids and looked at him. In her eyes he saw two large, silent tears . . .

★   ★   ★

Maspera finished the painting. A few light brushstrokes – a line here, a deepening of shadow there, a bit of touch-up for emphasis – and the work was done. Inside the ebony frame beamed a visionary figure of St. Cecilia playing the organ. The saint's upward, inspired gaze seemed to see the heavens unfolding before it and processions of angels descending; a face in contemplation of space, listening to the melodies of unseen choirs, while her hands, searching for a mystical chord, encompassed the keys with a masterful touch. The Count shifted his gaze from the painting to his wife and announced her liberation:

'It is complete.'

Bożena closed her eyes, weary from staring into space, leaned against the back of the chair and rested for a moment. Then she stepped down from the podium by the organ and stood beside her husband. Her eyelashes twitched nervously a couple of times, and her cheeks flushed with emotion.

'How beautiful she is!' a naïve impulse moved her to whisper.

'How could it be otherwise, Bożena? It is, after all, a stylized portrait of you.'

She looked at him sternly. 'You blaspheme, Henry. It's St. Cecilia. I just served as a model, to help you get closer to your remote ideal.'

'You are St. Cecilia to me, Bożena. That's how I want to have you always, as I cuddle and caress you in bed . . .'

'Only not now, Henry, not at this very moment, so beautiful for both of us,' she defended herself imploringly, having noticed the flame in his eyes. 'What you want to do now would be sacrilege. Can we not spend this solemn morning differently?'

But he was already sealing her lips with a burning kiss and tugging impatiently at her snow-white peplos.

'You'll regret this, Henry.' He barely heard her quiet complaint, muffled by his passion, and he plunged into the depths of amorous madness. This time, however, his blissful abandon did not last long. He was soon roused from his ecstasy by Bożena's alarming state. Her body, splayed out in total vulnerability to his lust on the torture-block of their marriage bed, suddenly in the midst of his caresses took on the appearance of a dead thing; her features hardened, glazed over with a patina of cadaverous yellow; her legs and arms stiffened; her lower parts constricted as if by the frost of death. A chill emanated from her. His hair bristling in horror, he pressed his ear to her breast . . .

There was no heartbeat.

'Bożena! Bożena!'

He pried her teeth apart and trickled a few drops of wine into her mouth. After a few minutes, she regained consciousness. Their gazes met; his – concerned and questioning, hers – austere and otherworldly.

* * *

A secret had crept into the private life of the Masperas. It had slipped inconspicuously through some half-open door and sat down unnoticed beside the hearth. Shadows of mystery spread throughout the castle. Day by day, the atmosphere of this seaside nook became imbued with a deepening sense of strangeness. The mundane reality of everyday life, immersed in this mysterious solution, took on the quality of a caricature; it mocked itself, like a face gazing into a concave mirror…

Bożena was reluctant to leave the castle, and even within it she confined herself to the bedroom and the library. She spent hours reading and did not like to be disturbed. The Count often had the impression that his wife wanted to hide from him whatever book she was absorbed in reading. Whenever he unexpectedly entered the library, Bożena would quickly put down the volume she had been holding and, having mixed it in among the other books on a nearby table, she would take up another and immerse herself in its contents with apparent interest. Maspera had the eyes of a lynx and took note of the format and binding of the volume. One night he crept into the library and found the book in a cabinet. It was a medieval treatise on magic, bound in elkskin, entitled *Speculum aeternitatis seu huius et alterius mundi reciprocum ligamentum – The Mirror of Eternity, or The Mutual Relationship Between This World and the Other*.

He opened the volume to page forty-seven, which Bożena had bookmarked. It was Chapter Ten, bizarrely titled: 'The Laws of Body and Soul Viewed through the Mystery of Exchange'.

The count's mouth twisted in a scornful smile. He replaced the book and tiptoed out of the library feeling wholly reassured, and resolved never to interrupt his wife's reading again. He was not afraid of 'mystical fantasies'. It never crossed his mind that there might be a connection between Bożena's increasingly strange behavior and the contents of the treatise.

And yet even the old burgrave once remarked to him on the countess's growing attachment to domestic life, unusual in those days.

'Don't worry about it, my old man,' he reassured him. 'She's obviously fine with it. Women will have their whims. One should not oppose them.'

If Maspera had observed his wife's lifestyle more carefully, he would have noticed still more changes in her character. Bożena began to show a particular affinity for certain objects and furnishings in the bedroom and library. The count would often find her in a chair by the window, tenderly running her hand over the amber knob of a paperweight, or letting her fingers wander over the Doric jug he had acquired years ago in Taormina during his travels in Sicily. In spite of his protests, she had taken to helping the servants dust the drapes and furniture, and she categorically insisted on watering the flowers herself. Bożena did not like for any member of the household to be in one of her favorite rooms, save for herself and her husband. The countess was protective of their atmosphere, as if she feared that strangers and neutral people would contaminate it with their presence.

Bożena's constant presence in these closed interior spaces created a mysterious symbiosis and mutual interpenetration between her and them. The countess gradually imbued these two gloomy Gothic chambers and everything within them with her personality. But they, too, did not fail to exert their own influence upon her.

Bożena felt that with each passing day she was becoming more deeply connected to them, as though some invisible force had been binding her, perhaps over the course of years, with unbreakable bonds to those vaulted halls, illuminated by the gloomy light of the stained glass windows through which sounded the deafening roar of the sea, along with the occasional cry of a stray seagull or the whistle of an autumnal gale. Sweetly and silently, with a bundle of keys and a stole whiter than snow, the castle's mistress moved through its rooms; sweetly and silently she submitted to her husband's will whenever he took her in his insatiable arms.

For Maspera's passion intensified as the years passed. Her passivity and lack of reaction only excited him more; the count still deluded himself that the heat of his fires would melt her virgin coldness and frigidity. The awareness that he was continually violating what was sacred in her added a sacrilegious charm to these acts. This charm was magnified to orgasmic proportions by the mysterious state into which, after several years together, Bożena constantly lapsed during these conjugal engagements.

The first time Maspera encountered this was on that memorable autumn morning, after finishing the painting of St. Cecilia. That was just a prelude. A few months later the symptom was repeated in a magnified form; Bożena's strange lethargic state lasted much longer this time, and only after an hour of attempting to rouse her did he manage to bring her back to consciousness. These attacks of torpor became more frequent, occurring at shorter intervals and lasting for longer periods. Sometimes the countess's body rested on the marital bed, stiff and cold as a corpse, for several hours.

At first, this state aroused a feeling of mortal fear in the count and curbed his erotic endeavours. With time, he became accustomed to these unusual symptoms and even found in them a source of perverse pleasure. The vulnerability of this chaste, virginal woman in her cold, deathlike state inflamed his passion to its utmost limits. He no longer even attempted to rouse her from her lethargic slumber, intentionally leaving that to the spontaneous action of her body in order to prolong these moments of ghoulish euphoria. The zenith of his elation occurred at the moment of her awakening when, beneath the passion of his lovemaking, the marble-white, cold body slowly, gradually, became tinted with the pink hue of blood, as the blessed fluid of warmth and life again began to flow through her arteries, and the heavy curtains of silken eyelashes were thrown open wide, exposing eyes that struck him with their astonishment and silent complaint . . .

And then something happened which cast an unwavering shadow of mystery over Maspera's life. On one occasion, this lethargic state stretched on excessively. Hours passed, and Bożena remained lying there, stiff, cold, and motionless. His most fervent efforts failed to revive her. After forty-eight hours, lifelessness had fully set in; the body looked like a corpse. The horror of death hung over the Masperas' marriage bed. The count was at his wits' end. He threw himself on his knees and, showering her with kisses, endeavored with the tenderest of entreaties and exhortations to turn her around on the path to eternity. He promised to change his ways, vowed never to touch her cherished body again. All in vain. Bożena would not awaken.

Maspera would not, could not, believe it. He locked himself in the bedroom with the deceased and did not allow anyone inside. He told the servants that the countess had fallen ill and did not want to be disturbed. Four dreadful days passed, and four even more dreadful nights. On the fifth, as he maintained his vigil beside the corpse and gazed at its beloved features under the silver light of the moon, he heard the sound of music in the adjoining room. He opened the door and saw Bożena playing the organ in the bay window in the corner of the room. She turned an inspired face toward him, smiled, and vanished. Now he no longer doubted that she had died.

He returned to the body and wrapped his arms around it in a farewell embrace. The odor of the corpse mingled with the cadaverous fumes of the candles into a spectral miasma that made his head reel. In the flames of grim lust, by the glow of the dying candles, he possessed her for the last time. Suddenly he felt a sharp pain; the dead woman's teeth had opened and sunk into his lips. Her eyelids slowly opened and the fire of life shot from her eyes. Her white arms encircled his neck, twisted around him like strands of ivy. A sound like the cooing of a turtledove emerged from her heaving breast and merged with his shouts into a bacchic duet of triumph.

'Bożena! Bożena!'

Her eyes shone with astonishment. She shook her head in protest:

'I am not Bożena. Look closely into my eyes!'

He looked and became convinced that the woman he was holding in his arms was not his wife. Someone else was looking at him through her eyes . . . From an otherworldly distance, he heard the voice of the dead woman for the last time in his life:

'Bożena has departed for the hereafter. She has left you here in the physical plane to watch over you in the spirit realm. And since you have loved my earthly form beyond measure and elevated it above the beauty of my soul, I leave you my body as a legacy. The higher will, acceding to my requests, has permitted the one whom you now caress to take up the corporeal shell which I have abandoned, and to dwell in it beside you as your wife. This exchange must remain a secret from the world, and therefore you shall call it by my name before men. But you should know that she belongs to the order of spirits incarnated for the first time, and therefore is eager to experience life and all that relates to it. Know also that it is to me she owes her shape, and that I am, in a way, her mother;

therefore, it is from me also that she will receive her proper name. In the intimacy of your amorous raptures, you will call her Morphena, that is, daughter of shape . . . Say goodbye to me, Henry, and live happily with her! Perhaps Morphena, clothed in the form of your first wife, can provide you with that true happiness that I, unfortunately, could not.'

These were Bożena's last words, her testament. Maspera obeyed her will and went out of the mourning chamber into the world with his lovely wife leaning on his arm. But he knew no more joy. Since that mysterious night, no smile has brightened his countenance. Gloomy, pensive, and prematurely gray, he would lock himself in the library and while away the hours there in solitude, admitting no one, not even his wife. Occasionally he would wander through the empty galleries of the castle, listening for the sound of elusive music. At times he would seem to be chasing someone, reaching out and grasping the invisible figure in a passionate embrace. Other times his wife would find him in the bay window by the organ, leaning over the back of the chair as though nuzzling his tear-streaked face against someone else's.

Morphena's passion did not soothe him; on the contrary, it intensified his longing for the other. Until one morning when, after a night of tumultuous emotions, he was found beside his wife with his skull shattered by a gunshot. He had set out on the path of eternity, to meet the Unforgotten One.

Szatera's Engrams

All around was nothing but empty space. As far as the eye could see, there were only stretches of railroad tracks, and telegraph poles jutting from the ground. When the wind died down for a moment, one could hear the subdued hum of the current moving through the wires, and when it picked back up again, replenished by a fresh gale, the chatter of the telegrams died down and the vast expanse let out a plaintive groan . . .

From time to time, yellow leaves flew off the trees along the roadside and, caught in the clutches of gale-force winds, fluttered over the embankment and disappeared down the other side, or rolled morosely over the tracks in a withered, rustling procession. Sheets of cloud spreading in the autumn twilight clothed the world in a dull gray. In a veil of mist, in a shawl of soft rain, quiet melancholy wandered through the fields . . .

Szatera drew his coat more tightly around him, lifted his collar and walked on. The stationmaster enjoyed his evening walks toward Kniejów at this time of day, when the weather becomes cloudy, contours blur, and the world is taken over by the kingdom of darkness. He liked this strange hour at the close of the day, when shadows cover the ground and a great secret is born. Every tree, every shrub, every windmill, and every stone in the fields assumes an air of mystery: alluring, enticing, deceiving. From the deepest reaches of the twilight, a nameless something leans out, stretches its slumber-cramped limbs, raises its head, smiles. A poor, neglected creature of the gray hour.

The stationmaster of Zaklicz understood its deep lyricism, for he felt that his own most profound, heartfelt tones flowed in sync with the melodies of dusk.

Ludwik Szatera was a lover of reminiscences, because he could never reconcile himself to the eternal passing of people, events, and things. Each moment, slipping irrevocably into the past, had a priceless value for him, and he bade farewell to each one with a feeling of ineffable regret. What he would have given to reverse its course on the path, to stop it from disappearing around the bend! And yet he knew that the sacrifice would be in vain, and that what was passing on could not be saved, so that, in the end, life became a rosary of partings and farewells, one great elegy swelling with unbounded lyricism, sung in the depths of a faithful heart to those things which have passed on, faded off into the distance . . .

For the past two years, at this twilight hour when the last scheduled train had departed and he was off duty until three in the morning, Szatera had been regularly taking walks in the same direction: towards the now-defunct stop in Kniejów. A year ago, the station building still stood there, with a switch tower at the entrance, as well as two semaphores and a pair of switch boxes. The manager of that station, which was a mere four kilometers from Zaklicz, had been one Droń, a friend of Szatera's who was a quiet, good-hearted man and an assiduous clerk. The stop at Kniejów, which was only used by freight trains, had actually been established as a transfer station for freight cars, which would be moved to a side track for a certain period before again being sent on their way.

This outpost, which existed for many years, had been abruptly shut down. Whether it had proved to be unnecessary, or could not be sustained without exceeding the railway budget, is unknown: suffice it to say that the authorities closed the station. Droń was transferred somewhere out near the eastern border, and the switchman Żak was reassigned to the station at Pochmarz. No trace remained of the former stop: the buildings had been completely dismantled, the facilities and signals removed. The fenced-in garden where he and his friend had whiled away so many evening hours had also disappeared, along with the side-rails where they had parked the freight cars. There was only a milestone a few steps away from the telegraph pole to indicate where the station used to be.

This stone, tangible proof of the life that once had been and now was no more, testament to events which had passed away forever, had become the object of Szatera's evening strolls. He typically set out from Zaklicz after the final train at five o'clock and reached the milestone in Kniejów after an hour's walk. Under the afterglow of the setting sun in summer and spring, and the deep gray haze in winter and late autumn, he would sit on this white remnant of the past and smoke his pipe in deep contemplation. At all times, he was faithfully accompanied by the melancholic feeling of the place and the great silence of the fields . . . When he returned to Zaklicz, to his home, it was always already quite dark . . .

And so had passed the first year following the closure of the station. His walks to Kniejów became indispensable, something he could not live without — they became 'second nature'. Szatera felt sick whenever some wretched circumstance came about to prevent him from taking this daily walk.

That is, until something occurred which seemed to reward him for his faithfulness of heart, fulfilling in an exceptional way the object of his extended longing . . .

It was a week before, on the memorable day of October 9.

As was his custom at around five o'clock in the evening, Szatera donned a fresh uniform, put on a newly acquired greatcoat adorned with his stationmaster's badges and, firmly setting his service cap in place, set off towards Kniejów. The evening was just as it was today, gloomy and dismal. Leaden clouds grappled with the winds overhead — rains lashed this way and that as though shaken through a sieve, while above the rattling of the gales there rose the occasional abrasive cries of wet crows and jackdaws.

The stationmaster walked along hurriedly, feeling more down and depressed than usual. The evening had stirred up in him a wave of recollections stronger than ever before. For that day was the anniversary of the station's decommissioning. He recalled as if it were yesterday the moment he last parted with his friend. As they were chatting, Droń had abruptly fallen silent and walked quickly towards the window, as if searching for something in the space outside. After a moment he turned and, shaking hands goodbye, said in a halting, stifled voice:

'Be well, old friend. I leave tomorrow.'

'Where to?' he asked anxiously.

'Out east – some godforsaken Cossack hellhole in the middle of nowhere.'

'Are you kidding?'

'Not at all. That's the order. They're shutting down my post tomorrow. No longer needed.' And having embraced him, Szatera pushed him almost violently through the doorway. The old codger was afraid he might begin sobbing in the presence of his companion and sought to defend himself against the prospect.

They started to dismantle the station the very next day . . . This happened a year ago, more or less at the same evening hour . . . Now that moment was returning on the wings of the autumn gale, in the whispering of withered leaves, in the melodies of the rain . . . The anniversary . . .

Szatera was approaching the area where the station had formerly stood. In the murky twilight, he could just make out the white shaft of the milestone. Then, upon looking up, he shuddered. From some distance ahead, above and to the right of the tracks, a signal beacon was shining in the darkness of the evening: a pair of large, yellow eyes.

'What's that? Some kind of semaphore redivivus?' He quickened his pace toward the signal, but as he reached the mile-marker, the lights suddenly went out. With a heavy heart, he began looking for the signal pole, but his search was in vain. It had, after all, been a year since it was removed.

'Where were those lights coming from, then . . . An illusion, or what the devil . . . ? Or maybe it was a bit past the station, on the other side?' And, having passed the milestone, he continued in the direction of Wygnanka. After a quarter of an hour, however, he still had not located the object of his search, so he turned back toward Kniejów.

'I must have been seeing things,' he decided, heading for his preferred stopping place.

But who could describe his amazement when he yet again observed, at a height of about six meters above him, a pair of signal lights glowing blood-red; the change in color warned that the space ahead was occupied.

Szatera rubbed his eyes once and then again, not believing what he was seeing: the apparition had not disappeared – the fiery lanterns suspended from the arm of the invisible semaphore still burned there above him. The stationmaster sat down on the stone and, lighting his pipe, stared at the warning signal as though hypnotized.

He did not recall how long he remained in this state of contemplation – perhaps an hour, perhaps two or three. When he came back to himself, darkness had settled in the east, and a gray frost blanketed the grass. The red lights had vanished; only the stiff black telegraph wires extended in the empty region of space above him.

Shivering with fever and chilled to the bone, yet with a strange feeling of bliss in his heart, Szatera returned with a brisk step to the station in Zaklicz to begin his morning shift.

A week had passed since that evening – seven unforgettable days in the stationmaster's life – seven days of miracles – seven days of communing face to face with the Nameless. Now every day he found the mysterious signals lit for him in Kniejów, the invisible semaphore in operation. Someone's caring hand hung rings of light in the space above, changed their colors, modulated their glow. And for those few days it seemed to Szatera that the good old days had returned, that the station would soon come back to life and he would hear again the booming voice of his friend from somewhere on the platform:

'Cars down to the last line! Set the third switch rail! Roll 'em onto the side track!'

For now it was only that pair of lights creeping quietly in the unraveling twilight, but soon, in a day, in two . . . he might have all of it back! . . .

Today, the 17th of October, the stationmaster of Zaklicz headed excitedly toward this place of memories. With bated breath he noted the distance he had covered by the mile markers and rushed ahead, carried on the wings of his desire. When he had passed the third roadside marker and reached his destination, he plunged his lynx-like gaze into the vastness above and did not take his eyes off it. But today he did not see the signal: the silent and soundless space was draped in autumnal blackness.

So he sat down on a stone and waited. He waited an hour, two, three; midnight passed, and he continued his vigil until dawn, but the lights never appeared. Finally, his head hung low, he headed back toward his own station with unsteady, drunken steps . . .

The next day, a horrible accident happened at Zaklicz. As a result of his own carelessness, a shunter named Jaksa fell under the wheels of a passenger car from Wygnanka and was torn to pieces. All that remained of his mercilessly ravaged body was his hand, which was thrown by the train onto the first track, just before the platform. The sight of this bloody human remnant, clad in the sleeve of a service uniform, with its five fingers splayed and a pale fragment of bone protruding, etched itself deeply into Szatera's memory. So, even though the station's crew quickly removed all traces of the accident and covered the place where Jaksa's hand had lain with fresh sand, it still loomed before the eyes of the Zaklicz stationmaster, bloody and predatory . . .

A few weeks later, while crossing the tracks in front of the station, he noticed a peculiar caprice of the wind. In a few places between the rails, sand rose from the ground in funnel-like shapes and, after briefly swirling around in one spot, each one began to stretch and extend towards the others. The larger funnel formed by this activity carried on a few paces further and, after revolving a few more times, collapsed again between the tracks.

Szatera approached the spot and noticed that the sand which had been carried by the collective effort of the whirlwinds had settled into what looked like the shape of a human arm. Looking more closely at the sculpture formed by this wind-chimera, Szatera felt something close to fear: this hand of sand with claw-like fingers spread apart, protruding as if from a sleeve, looked like a cast of Jaksa's hand. The resemblance was striking, down to the smallest detail.

As he stood there astonished, unable to take his eyes off the incredible phenomenon, footsteps rustled behind him. He turned and saw the assistant Derwicz coming towards him.

'What's that you're inspecting on the track, sir?' asked the young man, raising two fingers to his cap in a salute.

'A peculiar phenomenon, my friend,' answered Szatera, pointing to the sand. 'What do you think of this figure?'

'Which one? Where?'

'Oh, here, this pile of sand. Come now, have a better look at it.'

At that moment a fresh gust of wind blew through and scattered the ephemeral form.

'*Sacre bleu!*' cursed Szatera. It had been worth seeing, but his colleague had come a few seconds too late.

He explained to his colleague what he had witnessed. Derwicz listened with interest, but did not seem convinced.

'It could have been an illusion, sir,' he said finally, with a tinge of skepticism in his voice. 'Perhaps you were thinking about the accident that recently occurred at the station.'

Szatera only shrugged impatiently, but said nothing. He didn't care whether the assistant believed in the reality of what he had just seen.

Over the next few days, this capricious gathering-up of the sand by whirlwinds recurred at various points on the track, but more and more indistinctly and inaccurately. The cast of the hand was fragmentary and unfinished: first some fingers were missing, then the arm looked shortened at the elbow. In the ensuing weeks the phenomenon occurred only sporadically, at first every two days, then every three or four days, until finally it stopped completely.

During the same period he observed something similar at the site of the former station in Kniejów. The lights of the invisible semaphore appeared a few more times, at intervals of several days, each time growing weaker, until finally they faded out and never returned . . .

Then something in Szatera, too, faltered and expired. For some time he nurtured illusory fancies within his soul, and just as they were on the verge of realization, the treacherous mirage would dissipate before his eyes, and the all-encompassing drabness of everyday life would again reign supreme . . .

But slowly, the reassuring light of dawn began to shine through the darkness surrounding him. Amid the chaos of things and events, an idea began to germinate. At first puny and delicate, over time it grew to exuberant proportions and stifled everything else; its hundred-armed growths matured into a multitude of stubborn roots and branches, flexible and impossible to eradicate.

From that point on, Szatera lived for and by this thought alone. It overshadowed the entire horizon of his mind, forcing everything else into the shadows as things of lesser importance. Focused entirely on this signpost of salvation, he headed straight for it, wavering neither left nor right, not looking at anything or anybody. The stationmaster was venturing down a dreadful path . . .

Influenced by the strange symptoms he had observed in Kniejów and at Zaklicz station, he came up with his 'Theory of Engrams', the saving of the past.

Because over time, Szatera became convinced that nothing in the world disappears; that no event, no matter how trivial, is ever lost without a trace. On the contrary, everything is preserved and recorded. Where exactly, he wasn't sure. Perhaps on some metaphysical plane, in the Hindu akasha, in some astral ether, or invisible, cosmic fluid? Real-life events, having taken place in the arena of the visible world, probably seep into the space of the fourth dimension, fixing their image there on the astral film. These images of past affairs, metaphysical photographs recorded somewhere in the otherworldly realm, Szatera called 'engrams' of events.

These engrams, traces of facts and occurrences in the past, persist in a latent state on the plates of the netherworld like images of the physical world produced by light on glass or emulsion-coated paper. They persist – existing *in potentia* – waiting for an opportunity . . . to return to the sphere of the visible and repeat themselves as an echo.

Because events have their echoes just as voices and sounds do; they like to repeat and reproduce themselves several times – sometimes over centuries. Their engrams, taking advantage of a fortunate constellation caused by a partial return of the events that once triggered them, pass from a latent state into an active, empirical one: they activate themselves.

The vitality of an engram depends on the extent and quality of the modifications produced in the otherworldly sphere by the original event. Tragic events make the most lasting impressions, because these most powerfully agitate those realms from the other side. Engrams of trivial and insignificant events remain hidden without an echo, unless someone 'draws them out'.

For the primary role in the activation of the engram is played by human feelings, thoughts, and memories. Man can use his longing to bring the past from 'heaven' down to earth; by persistently circling around past events, his thoughts make it easier for them to return to the realm of reality: they evoke the echo.

This is why the 'reverberation' of past events is stronger the more deeply they are longed for, and the fresher the engram is. It is easier to draw out echoes of the more recent past.

The further back in time the event, the more difficult it is to restore. Engrams of things long past do not readily lend themselves to reproduction. It seems that as they move away from us in time, their power weakens. The tendency to return is strongest soon after the event has taken place; then it weakens, becomes diluted, and finally dies out.

Szatera experienced this with respect to two different incidents directly involving him: activated by his persistent thoughts, their engrams partially reconstructed these past moments on several occasions; but then, having exhausted themselves, they began to dim until they faded away to nothingness.

But Szatera wanted to have the past alive before his eyes, still pulsing with the blood of the here-and-now, eternally present; he wanted it constantly by his side, ready to be summoned at will, like a lover obedient to his every command. Meanwhile she, weary and exhausted, continually slipped out of his loving embrace and hid behind the curtains of the netherworld.

All that remained for him were anniversaries, those strange years, days, and hours when, thanks to a mysterious agreement between this world and the other, dead people, events, and things return 'from heaven to earth'. What brings them to us – the intensified longings and thoughts of the living, or the law of periodic recurrence based on Pythagorean numerical ratios hidden deep within the structure of the universe – is unknown. But it is certain that anniversaries resurrect the past by activating its engrams. The collective longing of a certain group of individuals undoubtedly has a greater power to 'draw out' than the mental effort of one person, no matter how extraordinary . . .

Therefore the Zaklicz stationmaster, who referred to the anni-

versary of these events as the Day of the Dead, decided to patiently
await their arrival. The power of his thoughts and longings was
only enough to draw out a few echoes because, like everything
else in this world, his spiritual power also had its limits. Now he
had to wait for the help of others, for the collective cooperation
of his fellow wanderers on the earthly plane who would, on the
anniversary of events so important to him, contribute to their res-
urrection with their thoughts and recollections . . .

Meanwhile, life cut short the agony of waiting and sent him the
gift of a terrible accident, capable of searing robust, lasting images
onto the photographic plates of the netherworld.

This was the unforgettable accident at Zaklicz station on July 8,
1920. As a result of a reprehensible mistake on the part of an official in tower no. 2, who issued an erroneous 'Clear Entry' signal
on the semaphore, a collision occurred between a passenger train
from Pochmarz and an express train from Wygnanka. The impact
of the latter on the passenger train, which had already stopped
beside the platform, was so violent that both machines, having
forced their way into each other's bodies, collapsed one into the
other and formed a chimerical alloy bristling with convulsively
twisted stumps of iron. Eight cars of the passenger train and ten
of the express train were completely destroyed; all that remained
of them was a savage tangle of wood and iron, interspersed with
mangled human remains.

The casualties were enormous: almost the entire staff of the
express train was killed, along with ten officials working the passenger train and one hundred passengers.

For the next few days, the Zaklicz station looked like a hospital
or a battlefield. The moaning and groaning of victims sounded
from all around, the cloying smell of iodoform was in the air, and
the bloodstained white coats of doctors and surgeons could be seen
moving about on the platforms and in the waiting rooms. Szatera
would pace from one end of the station to the other looking like a
nervous wreck, at times anxiously plugging his ears, or lock himself in his station office. No one felt the catastrophe as profoundly
as he did. He became haggard and gaunt, like a skeleton walking
among the living.

But if someone had been able to look into his soul at that time, it would be apparent that the terrible accident had etched only certain, very precise details into it. One of them was the image of the engine driver who was driving the express train – an image that preceded the moment of the collision by a few seconds. Szatera saw the man's face at the critical instant – a gray, rather sallow face with eyes bulging out of their sockets – and followed the movement of his hand clenched in a hopeless effort around the brake lever. Then, at the very last second, he noticed something he could never quite make sense of. The driver suddenly smiled, took his hand off the lever and waved it dismissively. At the same time another human figure which resembled the driver, though its outlines were somewhat blurred, appeared next to him as though having sprouted from the train platform and, with the same dismissive smile, turned away from the boiler and began to descend the steps . . . At that moment came the explosive impact . . .

Amid the hellish crashing and banging, among the chaos of piled-up cars, and the intertwined mass of machines, people, and objects, the form of a young lady in a red scarf flashed before Szatera's eyes. The poor girl had tried to save herself by leaping out the window of one of the compartments. But her leap proved fatal, as she struck her head on one of the lamp posts and died on the spot . . . Then came the culminating moment – the most horrible of all, with its grisly charm . . .

Flung out from under one of the car's wheels, like an iron gear from one of the transmission belts, the head of a beautiful girl with bright, golden blond hair landed on the ground and rolled towards him. Suddenly he saw at his feet a pair of gorgeous violet eyes, already glazed over with the sheen of death, and a pair of parted lips like rose petals. Szatera bent down to this brutalized head, picked it up carefully in both hands as if it were a saintly relic and pressed its faded lips against his . . .

Right then, he felt pain and tasted blood. Her clenched teeth, small and pearly white, had opened at the moment of his kiss and closed again in a spasm of agony. Szatera tore his lip free of this amorous bond and let go of his lover's head with a shudder of horror. His vision went dark, the world began to spin under his feet, and he collapsed senselessly onto the rails. When he regained consciousness, the dead and wounded were already being carried away . . .

A month after the disaster, its gloomy echoes began to resonate at the station in Zaklicz.

It began with strange shadows on the walls of the warehouses near Track One. Szatera first noticed them on August 10th, as the freight train from Zwijachel was passing through. The shadows cast by the cars as they passed the buildings did not correspond to them at all in size or shape; what he saw on the warehouse walls looked more like the projection of a crude barricade than the shadow of cars in the typical alignment; their contours, normally rectangular and symmetrical, broke down in this shadowy reflection into a jagged, distorted line full of cracks, faults, and ruptures.

Strangest of all was the shadow of the steam-powered coal-car: in this capricious rendering, the machine appeared to have doubled; one could clearly distinguish a pair of smokestacks. The overall projection of the train gave the impression of a malicious caricature . . .

This first symptom, which repeated itself at intervals of a few days at a time, left Szatera much to contemplate. But there were soon to come other, more meaningful signs . . .

One evening at the end of August, Szatera observed a puzzling phenomenon with the arrival of a passenger train from Żuławy. As the train pulled slowly into the station, it seemed to him taller and more slender than usual. Staring more closely at the uppermost part of the cars, he soon discovered the reason. The train had a subtle but, to him, just quite discernible aura, which was, as it were, an upward extension of itself. This delicate superstructure, woven of vague, tenuous material, made the cars look taller than ever.

Szatera did not hesitate to share his observations with Derwicz.

'Look there, Derwicz,' he said to the station assistant, who was standing beside him. 'Does anything about that strike you as odd?'

And he indicated the train which, having emitted great puffs of steam from its gills, had meanwhile come to rest on the third track before the platform.

The assistant glanced over the whole line from the first car to the last and shook his head.

'I don't see anything unusual about it. Normal staffing, average load. Everything's in order.'

'Don't the cars seem a bit more slender than usual?' Szatera prompted.

The young man's eyes passed over the train once again, then settled on his superior with a look of bewilderment.

'It's an illusion, sir,' he answered calmly. 'A kind of optical illusion brought on, I suppose, by the atmospheric conditions today. There's been a good deal of fog in the air.'

'In that case, you would be subject to it, too.'

'Well, not necessarily. The individual properties of our visual organs also play a role.'

'Ha, ha, ha,' laughed Szatera derisively, 'in other words, you mean that each of us sees differently. Ha, too bad – I won't insist on the point. Perhaps my eyesight is a little different than others'.' And he gave the hand signal to depart . . .

At the beginning of September, the echoes began to assert themselves more vigorously. Almost every day during the week of September 3rd to the 10th, an unwarranted panic broke out among the passengers of the express train from Wygnanka. The moment the train pulled up at the Zaklicz station the terrified travelers packed in before the windows of the cars and crowded on the platforms, apparently wanting to get off as quickly as possible. A few of the most anxious ones jumped out as the train was still moving toward the station.

The hysteria reached its climax on September 9, when a brutal fight broke out among the passengers in one of the compartments as the train pulled in. A group of men with their canes raised had begun to force their way toward the exit, where a group of frightened women and children were gathered. By the time the train stopped alongside the platform, three windows and a couple of doors had been broken. One could hear women screaming frantically and children crying from inside the cars. A few people tumbled down the steps of the carriage, sustaining serious injuries in some cases, and others jumped from the windows with no concern for the consequences. When at last the train stopped and a vexed Derwicz began to inquire in a raised voice about the cause of the panic, the poor passengers could not give a definite answer. Helpless and stunned, they looked around at one another, blaming others who were still in the train. Someone shouted, 'We're going to crash!', someone else, 'Brace for impact!', setting off the panic. Derwicz could not sort out the truth, despite his earnest attempts.

Only for Szatera was the whole thing abundantly clear. He would have been surprised, even, if things had been otherwise. But this time he kept his peace and did not rush to offer an explanation.

Remarkable was the fact that each time, the panic had broken out only in the same two cars. These were numbers 232 and 135, which, having both escaped destruction in the July collision, had been incorporated into the new 'lineup'. Compelled by a strange feeling, Szatera had memorized the numbers of the surviving cars and written them down in the station logbook immediately after the disaster. There was no question of any mistake, because his notes confirmed these were the exact same cars. Even so, he made no mention of this to anyone, keeping the observation to himself.

What would be the point? Derwicz, the man closest to him by profession and common interests, was of a sober-minded nature and lacked sensitivity to the mysterious. Several attempts on his part to initiate Derwicz into awareness of the netherworld had failed completely. He would undoubtedly scoff at him now, blaming the 'alleged' symptoms on 'mere coincidence', 'chance', or some other banality. Szatera understood that he was doomed to complete solitude and that everything must remain his exclusive secret until the end.

All the more reason to keep another, even less believable observation to himself. At the height of the panic, a lady in a red shawl had leaned out from the window of one of the cars. Szatera recognized the woman at once. It was the same face, framed by luxuriant black hair, that he had first seen during the catastrophe two months before – the same wild eyes, searching in vain for rescue, the same white, anxious hands tightly clutching the window frame, beyond which only death awaited her. Now this woman was reprising her tragic role . . .

She looked so much like that other woman that Szatera went inside the carriage every time she appeared and searched for her to confirm with his own eyes. But his search was always fruitless. She was not in any of the compartments, nor in the neighboring cars, and could not be found anywhere on the entire train. The lady in the red shawl, having appeared once for a brief moment in the window of one of the doomed cars, always vanished without a trace . . .

And yet, the engram had not been actualized to its potential. The repetition did not satisfy Szatera's longing – his vast, boundless longing for her, the golden-haired one . . . The memory of the kiss trailed behind him with a refrain of painful delight, insisting on an echo . . .

O sweet, virginal lips! Greedy, bloodthirsty! . . .

Day after day he waited for his beloved to appear; day after day he looked out for her beautiful specter. His longing eyes raced over the windows of the cars, wandered over the faces of the passengers, peered into the compartments, but all in vain. They could not trace even the faintest shadow of that beloved head, could not seize upon the most subtle hint of its outline. The jealous otherworld, having consumed its victim, was unwilling to give it back to him . . .

Meanwhile, the echoes of the catastrophe seemed to be exhausting themselves. His heart heavy with despair, Szatera saw that with each passing day the repetitions grew weaker, the outlines blurry and less defined. After the 10th of September, they became less frequent, less accentuated, until by the middle of the month they finally ceased altogether. The atmosphere at the Zaklicz station soon returned to 'business as usual', to the relief of Derwicz and the delight of the staff, whose nerves had been frayed by the recent events.

Only the stationmaster was sad and gloomy. His soul was filled with feelings of profound emptiness and isolation which weighed down his formerly spry figure. The connection between this world and the next had been broken for an indefinite period. All that remained was his pain, faithful companion through the lonely hours, and the longing for his beloved, steadily eating away at the bonds of his spirit . . .

It was then, in the suffering-wracked depths of himself, that the germ of a diabolical idea emerged. His brain, convulsed with inner torment, began to inquire into the cause of the gaps and vague suggestions in the echoes of the last collision. Why were only certain details replayed? Why had the actualized engram omitted others? Why had the tragic image of her beloved head not returned? . . .

Maybe the conditions for its reproduction were inadequate? . . . And if so, perhaps they could be intensified? . . . Here, the frantically spinning wheels of his thoughts stopped for a moment. A shudder of horror ran through his body, and Szatera hesitated before coming to a final decision . . . But not for long. The overpowering allure of the beyond broke through the barrier of his scruples and dragged him behind it down the path to perdition. The stationmaster decided to provoke another collision, which would allow him to glimpse yet again, if only for a moment, a vision of that fair-haired girl . . .

The callous idea came to him one sleepless night, amidst the whistling of the autumn wind and the murmur of the telegraphic lines. It would be simple and straightforward to carry out. All he needed to do was hold one train a little longer at Zaklicz, while simultaneously sending a message to Pochmarz permitting the second train to leave on the same track. A matter of ten minutes. A collision was inevitable.

Szatera set about implementing his plan with bold enthusiasm. He chose a cloudy, October day, resonant with the lamentations of the wind and of dispirited birds.

Around five o'clock in the afternoon, when dusk had already cast its black net over the region, Szatera took over the assistant's duties. Twenty minutes later, a passenger train from Rakszawa pulled in. The stationmaster went out onto the platform and calmly inspected the carriages. He waited for the post to arrive and, without giving the signal to depart, returned to the station office.

From there, he could observe the situation comfortably through the window.

Soon several of the officials began to show signs of impatience. Having closed the doors of the carriages, the conductors repeat-

edly raised their flashlights to signal readiness for departure, and
the train manager stood with his trumpet to his mouth, awaiting
the return of the chief and the hand signal to release the train ...

It was high time now. In ten minutes, the express train from
Pochmarz would be arriving on the same track. Ten minutes!
Exactly as much time as it would take for the express to traverse
the space between the two stations, and for the passenger train to
reach the nearest fork in the tracks, from which it could switch
over to the safe rail.

But the stationmaster did not leave his office. His iron will split
into two, and was operating on dual fronts: here he was delaying
the train's departure, and there he was reaching with his murderous hand for the telegraph machine, to send his pernicious message
to the Pochmarz station ...

He fingered the button of the telegraph and pressed ...

Suddenly his hand went numb. Paralyzed by some obscure
force, his arm froze in the position in which he had just placed it.
He was overcome by a peculiar drowsiness, his limbs constrained
by a strange inertia. He felt something inside himself begin to sep-
arate, disconnect, break away. He stared out through the window
and *saw his own figure standing on the platform* ... It moved swiftly
towards the head of the train, into the circle of light cast by the station lamps, and abruptly raised its hand into the air ... An anxious
trumpet call sounded, and the train began to pull away ...

Through the window he watched the carriages plunge readily
into the darkness; saw how the machine, eager to make up for the
delay, tore through space at high speed; how the train, released
from its tether, escaped from its perilous standstill with each burst
of steam from its pistons ... Saved! ...

Szatera awoke as if from a deep sleep. His fingers, no longer
numb, nervously grasped the knob of the machine and resumed
the interrupted activity ... The signals began to pulsate. The
stationmaster took his hand off the instrument and rushed out
onto the platform like a whirlwind.

'Why has the passenger train from Rakszawa already left?' he
asked the first official menacingly.

'I don't understand, sir,' the man answered.

'What do you mean, you don't understand?' Szatera shouted, almost losing his composure. 'I'm asking who let the passenger train depart from the station?'

The subordinate stared at his superior, dumbfounded.

'You yourself were standing there, sir, when the train was dispatched,' he said finally, not quite understanding what was going on.

'I released that train? I myself? . . . That's impossible.'

'I saw it with my own eyes, just a few minutes ago. You were standing right there, sir, under that lamppost, and you gave the signal to depart. Just in time, thank goodness. The train was held up five minutes too long, anyway. The express from Pochmarz was just about to come into view. The departure bells were already sounding.'

Szatera ran his hand over his forehead.

'Unbelievable,' he whispered, his vision fixing upon the empty space. 'Unbelievable.'

And he walked slowly along the tracks in the direction from which the express train was approaching.

He could hear it already. The ground was already giving off a dull rumble, the rails were clattering . . . At the bend, where the main track branched off into a criss-crossed network of rails, the eyes of the machine flashed; huge, golden eyes that swelled and bulged into ever-expanding circles of light . . .

The stationmaster stopped between the tracks and leaned his back against the switch box, waiting. A rumbling filled his ears, a mist shrouded his eyes . . .

As the locomotive approached from a distance of several meters, he looked down and beheld – below the panting breast of the monster, between the fixtures of the headlights – *her head*. Gorgeous azure eyes looked at him, smiling gratefully, and her lips – those bloodthirsty, virginal lips – tempted him with the promise of pleasures . . .

That smile, those lips – they were calling to him. With arms outstretched, he charged beneath the wheels, down between the headlights, to reunite with his beloved forever . . .

Printed in the USA
CPSIA information can be obtained
at www.ICGtesting.com
LVHW090818221023
761714LV00028B/140